Oberlin College

Annual Reports

1897

Oberlin College

Annual Reports
1897

ISBN/EAN: 9783741198830

Manufactured in Europe, USA, Canada, Australia, Japa

Cover: Foto ©Andreas Hilbeck / pixelio.de

Manufactured and distributed by brebook publishing software
(www.brebook.com)

Oberlin College

Annual Reports

ANNUAL REPORTS.

PRESS OF
PEARCE, RANDOLPH & CO.,
OBERLIN, OHIO.
1898.

OBERLIN COLLEGE.

ANNUAL REPORTS FOR 1897.

Presented to the Trustees at the Annual Meeting, March 9, 1898.

REPORT OF THE CHAIRMAN OF THE FACULTY.

To the Board of Trustees :—

GENTLEMEN: Once more, in our lack of a president, the duty of making a general report falls upon the writer.

The organization of the College remains substantially the same as at the last annual report, ex-President Fairchild still acting as president of the Board of Trustees, the writer remaining Chairman of the Faculty, and the various standing committees being as shown upon a separate leaflet.

RESIGNATIONS.

At the close of the last College year, in June, two professors in the College Department terminated their work of instruction with us — Professor Churchill and Professor Kelsey. Professor Churchill's appointment dated back to 1858, when he was put in charge of the Mathematics and Physics. In 1890 he relinquished the Mathematics, and his department became that of Physics and Astronomy, although he had previously carried the Astronomy, as well as the other subjects. His term of service was forty years, lacking one. The resolutions that were passed upon his retirement, both by the trustees and the faculty, are a testimony to the rare intellectual and personal qualities which he had manifested in his long period of service, and

3

which had gained for him the admiration and love of so many generations of students.

Professor Kelsey's appointment to the chair of Botany dated from 1893, and he held the position for four years, resigning last summer to accept the pastorate of the Central Congregational Church in Toledo. His able and generous service has also been recognized, and there are further words of appreciation in the report of his successor, herewith printed.

We do not place ex-President Fairchild upon the list of those who have laid down their work. If he should fail to give any lectures in Theology this year, it will be due to the transfer of his lectures from the middle year to the senior year in the Seminary upon the inauguration of Professor King's work. The present senior class has already had work with him in this subject, and it is expected that next year he will give a course to the next senior class. Up to the time of his recent departure for the South he continued to act as chairman of the Prudential Committee, where his knowledge of the whole history and business of the College has been of the greatest value.

Edward D. Roe, Associate Professor of Mathematics since 1892, has been granted a leave of absence.

APPOINTMENTS.

The following appointments were made during the year:

Charles Edward St. John, Ph.D., was appointed Associate Professor of Physics and Astronomy for two years.

Herbert Lyon Jones, A.M., was appointed Associate Professor of Botany for two years.

Simon F. MacLennan, Ph.D., was appointed Instructor in Psychology and Pedagogy for two years. A separate leaflet, describing the preparation of the three preceding appointees, was printed and is distributed currently with the catalogues.

Rev. Henry Churchill King, D.D., was transferred from the chair of Philosophy in the College Department to that of Theology in the Theological Seminary.

Fred Monroe Tisdel, A.M., was reappointed Associate Professor of Rhetoric and Oratory for one year.

Cleveland King Chase, A.M., was reappointed Instructor in Latin for one year.

Frank Hardy Lane, Ph.B., was reappointed Assistant in Elocution and English Composition for one year.

Miss Eva May Oakes was reappointed Instructor in Drawing and Painting for two years.

WORK OF THE YEAR.

We have had another year of exceptional success in the work of instruction and study, which is the great end for which the College exists.

The spirit of earnest work has pervaded every department, among both instructors and students. There has been harmony in our counsels, and a high standard of effort and conduct on the part of the students. The current of College life has been a full and varied one, and its flow has been in favorable directions. Aside from matters purely scholastic, there have been favorable experiences in social matters, favorable progress in the literary societies, in oratorical and debating contests, in the departmental clubs and seminars, in athletic enterprises, in musical undertakings, in public courses of lectures, in religious and missionary organizations, and in various lines of activity in which student energy will spend itself. There has been good feeling between faculty and students, one incident in which was a formal vote of thanks to the faculty by the Athletic Association, for the supervision and liberal interest in athletics which had been shown by the faculty.

POLICY.

In the absence of a President, the management of the internal affairs of the College has necessarily been by faculties and committees, but in this respect there has been no especial change from the liberal policy that had previously been pursued under President Ballantine, President Fairchild and their predecessors. The responsibilities that are laid upon members of the faculty necessitate discussion of policies, promote the feeling that every one has a voice, engender a feeling of loyalty to the final decision, and result in a wiser and steadier policy than would otherwise be secured. Undoubtedly more moral power is developed in the faculty by this exercise of responsibility; and this is a matter of great importance in a college which endeavors to mould character as well as to train the minds of students. This plan makes constant demands upon the time of the instructors, and it takes time for a new appointee, trained under different surroundings, to come into the fullest sympathy with the aims of the College, and to contribute his best offerings to its policy and life; but the great importance of the result justifies the expenditure, and should make us slow in altering the plan.

THE COUNCIL.

In this connection, it should be said that the Council, which consists only of the older and permanent appointees, has proved by experience to be a valuable feature of our organization, for the discussion of questions like appointments and the budget. It is efficient because of its smaller numbers, and still educative and co-ordinating, because it brings the details of the financial condition of the College to the knowledge of so large a number.

The Council membership is now smaller than hitherto, on account of the recent retirement of several full professors, and our system of probation in new appointments. A large number of important new appointments have been made within the last two years, and this is an element in our situation that needs to be carefully borne in mind.

THE PRESIDENCY.

The desirability of the appointment of a president at as early a day as possible is strongly felt by the faculty, and doubtless by the trustees and all our constituency as well. While no feeling of urgency in the matter should be allowed to embarrass the committee in its difficult task, we must all realize that in our relations to the outside public, in our relations to our friends in all parts of the country, in our relations to our financial problem, as well as to our work within the College, we must suffer some detriment until the presidential problem is successfully solved.

There are some questions involving the relations between faculty and students and some customs that have prevailed here for a long time, concerning which the faculty have been uncertain whether it was better to discuss them now, or to leave them for the next administration to deal with. In some of these points it might be a relief to the future administration to have them settled before it is inaugurated.

ATTENDANCE.

While the total attendance of students does not vary greatly from that of last year (the exact figures are not yet compiled), one feature which is sometimes remarked upon is the preponderance of the number of women over that of men. The visitor at chapel sometimes notes this. Upon comparing the enrollments for the past five years, however, it is found that the percentage has not been changing. It stands at 54 per cent., rising one year to 55 per cent. in the total enrollment. If we exclude the Conservatory, where the proportion of women to men is approximately five to one, it will be found that in the literary departments there has been a distinct excess of men. In the College classes, however, the last catalogue shows that there are as many women as men — 214 out of 428 — and there has been a gain of women for three years. On the other hand, if we go back to 1892-3, and count the women of the third and fourth years of the Literary course as College students, we shall find that the women lacked only 16 of equaling the men in numbers that year. It seems to be true that, throughout the country, more women are going to college than formerly. At Chicago and other universities the numbers are increasing. Oberlin has perhaps fewer formidable competitors for women students than she has for men. We ought to consider what we can do, in equipment, in living accommodations and in policy, to assist in maintaining the desired preponderance of men.

WOMEN AS PROFESSORS.

Does the presence of so many College women make it fitting that there should be some women professors? We have for many years had two women professors, Mrs. Johnston, who adds to her duties as dean the chair of Mediæval History, and Miss Wattles, who teaches Piano and Harmony

6

in the Conservatory. Now there comes from the faculty a recommendation for the appointment of a woman, qualified by scholarship and successful experience, to a permanent position in charge of a modern language in the College Department, and of another, equally qualified, as associate professor of Latin in the Academy. The policy is not a new one. The trustees have already agreed to accept and administer a professorship endowment, raised by women, with the agreement that a woman professor shall be the beneficiary. While it may not be best to carry this policy far, we should congratulate ourselves that we have such accomplished candidates in the service of the College.

LECTURES.

Quite a large number of public lectures and addresses have been given by members of the faculty, outside their regular College work, both in Oberlin and in other places. The Thursday lecture has become a monthly instead of a weekly occasion, and about half the lectures are given by members of the faculty. A number of articles in standard journals have been contributed, and a number of papers presented at scientific and educational gatherings by members of the faculty, some of which are mentioned in their individual reports.

THE MASTER'S DEGREE.

A recommendation comes from the faculty, modifying, in one particular, the terms upon which the degree of A. M. should hereafter be granted. In comparing the practice in universities East and West, it is found that in some Western institutions there is a tendency to require for this degree the same quality of original investigation, though less in amount, that is required for the degree of Doctor of Philosophy. This can hardly be said of most of the Eastern institutions, where the doctor's degree is very carefully given.

ACKNOWLEDGEMENTS.

Attention should be drawn to a number of benefactions mentioned in the reports of individual professors, which are printed herewith. We are especially fortunate in the decision of General Cox to make his residence in Oberlin, to give his library to the College Library, and to continue here his literary work upon the Military History of the War. The students and citizens have had the privilege of hearing an address from him, on Washington's birthday, recounting impressively the sufferings and the patriotism of the army in East Tennessee in the winter of 1863-4, which furnished a modern parallel to the conditions at Valley Forge in 1777-8.

The helpfulness of the Students' Library Association (U. L. A.) is mentioned by the Librarian, and is gratefully recognized by the faculty. They spent as much money for the purchase of books last year as did the College Library.

7

Professor Jewett mentions the generosity of Rev. R. T. Cross, of the class of 1867, in the matter of his collection of minerals.

Professor Jones mentions the gift of the very large and valuable herbarium of Professor F. D. Kelsey, upon his retirement, but he is too modest to state that most of the other series enumerated were his own gift to the College, as he comes to enter upon his labors here.

OUTSIDE REPRESENTATION.

This work takes many different channels, such as advertising, press notices, representation at alumni associations and various educational gatherings, etc. Principal J. F. Peck, of the Academy, will spend the coming spring term in visiting high schools. It is questionable whether our outlays in this general line of outside representation have not been curtailed quite as much as they will bear to be.

SUMMER SCHOOL.

The last summer's session was the first under the new management. Some success attended the efforts to draw in public school teachers, but it is believed and planned that much more shall be done in the future sessions. As previously stated, its accounts are kept separate, and will not be allowed to intrench upon the College treasury.

SCHOLARSHIPS.

A proposition comes from the faculty, by which they are to do what they can in the way of replacing the " Trustee Scholarships " with a loan fund, from which students near graduation may borrow, repaying the amounts after five years. As fast as this fund can be raised by subscription, the payments on the Trustee Scholarships, which payments amount to about $1,800 per year, are to be reduced and discontinued. All reductions on this plan will result in the addition of equal amounts to our income available for other purposes.

The total amount of our endowed scholarships is very meager compared with those possessed by many competing colleges, and are very far short of our needs.

CHANGES IN THE SEMINARY.

I would direct especial attention to the general report of the Theological Seminary, in which a number of important changes are described, such as the dropping of the English course, raising the standard of admission, changing the order of studies, the recommendation of a four-year course, etc. While the immediate result of these changes may diminish somewhat the number of students, it is believed that the quality of the work will be eventually recognized, and the results will prove the wisdom of the steps taken.

The needs in the various departments for better equipment are stated in the individual reports. The unanimity of the call for more books for the library, especially such as can be selected by the instructors themselves, cannot fail to strike the attention of the trustees.

But the most serious attention needs to be given to plans for increasing at once the income of the College. In the very severe efforts which have been made, during these past few years, to make the expenditures and income meet, the pressure upon the faculty has been to reduce expenses, and to invent and practice economies. They have studied their problem hard, and the expenditures have been reduced by many thousands of dollars. If there has been failure to reach a balance, it is not due to expenditures beyond the approved estimates, but to a failure of the College to receive the estimated income; so it would seem as if we could not rightly meet the present situation without the most earnest planning to secure immediate additions to our income, and thus bring up the other side of the account. While such efforts cannot but be more or less involved with the question of the presidency, yet independently of that question there are many steps that can be taken, and in which we cannot afford any further delay. Compared with these, all the other items in these reports must seem of trivial importance.

Respectfully submitted,

ALBERT A. WRIGHT.

9

REPORT OF THE LIBRARY DEPARTMENT.

To the Chairman of the Faculty :—

SIR: The report of the Treasurer of the College gives a full statement of the receipts and expenditures on account of the Library. The indebtedness for general expenses, the cause of which was fully explained in my last report, has been still further reduced, as is shown by the following table:

Advances to the Library—General Expenses.

1893	$1,798.88	1896	$1,243.99
1894	1,405.82	1897	1,114.99
1895	1,586.05		

Each year it becomes increasingly difficult to save anything out of the small income available for general expenses. As the Library increases, an increase of expenses is inevitable. The cost of the annual inventory, of binding — and especially of rebinding — of keeping order on the shelves, and of similar items of expense, is directly affected by the increase of books, while other items, such as replacing books on shelves, are indirectly affected by means of the increased distances to be traveled. The Library now has books on five floors of the building, and though they are as conveniently disposed as is possible until the entire building is available for Library purposes, still the labor of replacing books on the shelves is very much increased. Where this work in former years was performed by the girls at the delivery desk, it is now necessary to employ a boy some hours each day. This is but a single illustration among many which might be given, from which the Trustees will see that an increase in the running expenses of the Library is inevitable. I will only add that a very considerable increase in this direction is urgent in order to do well the work we are now attempting, but the financial condition of the College is such that we feel obliged to make the present force suffice.

INCOME FOR BOOKS ALTOGETHER INADEQUATE.

The most pressing need of the Library, however, is money with which to purchase books. The total *regular* income of the Library, available for books, was last year only $698.57. Of this amount $49.50, owing to conditions attached to the deed of gift, or other reasons, was not available to supply the needs of the instructors, thus leaving only $650. Of this amount, about $350 is required to keep up periodicals, annuals, cyclopædias, and other continuations already taken by the Library. Thus the amount which is really available to be used in purchasing books *urgently* needed by instructors for themselves and their students is only $300, which, if distributed among the twenty-eight departments of instruction to which appropriations have usually been made, will permit each professor to select books to the amount of $10 each year for the enlargement of the Library in his department. It is hopeless to attempt to express, in adequate words, the utter insufficiency of this sum, and the impossibility of furnishing instruction suited to modern methods, if this situation continues.

I am not sure that the Trustees realize that this is a new situation, brought about in part by the withdrawal of a portion of the Library endowment, but chiefly by the steady decline in the rate of interest. If new endowments are not speedily received, it will be necessary to ask for appropriations from the Trustees; $1,000 a year would be as little as would suffice, for we ought to have $5,000 a year if the Library is to become what it is said elsewhere to be, "the heart of the university." An endowment reaching $200,000, half for running expenses, half for books, would do more to establish Oberlin on a firm foundation as an institution of higher learning than any other single gift. It would bring great relief to the College by providing for the cost of binding, heat, light, maintenance of the building, and other current expenses, and would greatly encourage every teacher and pupil. Cannot some rich and generous friend of the College be found whose love for Christian education, and for the things for which Oberlin has stood, will prompt him to provide, in whole or in part, for this great need?

ADDITIONS FOR THE YEAR.

Returning to the work of the past year, there is much to encourage us. At the beginning of the year the Library contained 35,219 volumes and 19,125 pamphlets. During the year there were added 1,924 volumes, and 2,980 pamphlets were catalogued, making the total at the end of the year 37,143 volumes and 22,105 catalogued pamphlets. There are, besides the catalogued pamphlets, a large number, estimated as 20,000, of pamphlets uncatalogued; but as it is impossible to tell how far these will prove to be additions, they are not included. The increase in bound volumes was made up of books given (:,061) and books purchased (863). Of those purchased, the various funds supplied the following numbers: Holbrook, 280; gift of E. A. West, 108; Harkness, 96; Wrisley, 71; Plumb, 55; Class of 1885, 43; Grant, 42; Keep Clarke, 30; other funds, from 1 to 19 each. Among donors, the following should be mentioned as having given many volumes: E. A. Andrews, W. G. Ballantine, Prof. C. H. Churchill, '52 Theo.; Miss Elizabeth De-Witt of Elyria, Prof. F. D. Kelsey, M. M. Longley, '60; I. S. Metcalf of Elyria, Mrs. C. V. Spear, and Prof. A. A. Wright. Mrs. E. W. Lord and

Rev. D. L. Leonard, D. D., have, as in former years, given many pamphlets and unbound periodicals.

During the year the Library was open 293 days, and 14,670 books were drawn for home use. The number of readers during the year was 69,060, an average of 235 for each day throughout the year. As this includes vacation periods, the general average for the year is much smaller than the actual average during term time. Thus, in February, 1897, the Library was open 23 days, with total number of readers for the month of 8,631, or a daily average of 375. Eleven hundred and thirty-five persons drew books for home use during the year. About 100 of these were officers of the College or citizens of the town. It thus appears that 1,035 students out of 1,283 connected with the College during the year drew books from the Library for home use. Probably nearly all the others made use of the Library, but without drawing for home use.

The cataloguers have during the past year classified, shelf-listed and catalogued 1,691 bound volumes and 3,149 pamphlets, a total of 5,110, a number just about equalling our accessions. There remain, however, about 4,000 bound volumes and 20,000 pamphlets still uncatalogued. A thorough revision of a portion of the shelf-lists was made necessary by the removal of some 10,000 volumes to the lower or museum floor, as described in my last report, and as a result 785 bound volumes and 109 pamphlets were withdrawn from the stacks for trifling corrections. During the year 7,284 new cards were written and placed in the catalogue, 1,878 cards were corrected for new additions, and 1,359 cards were changed to correspond with the corrections required as a result of the revision of the shelf-lists.

Six hundred and sixty-four volumes have been sent to the binder, of which 220 were volumes sent for repairs, while the remainder was new work.

The gift by General Jacob D. Cox of his valuable private library, though not formally made during the period covered by this report, was the occasion of certain important improvements, which were undertaken near the close of the summer vacation, and should therefore be mentioned. The cases carried into the museum the previous summer were rearranged, and new ones were constructed over an area of equal extent, and a second story placed over all. In the northeast corner of the ground floor a small but well-lighted room was arranged, which is occupied by General Cox as a study. Under the terms of gift, the volumes are to be kept in proximity to this room, so long as General Cox may require them. From the upper story of this newly-constructed stack, a stairway communicates with the main reading room, thus rendering all the volumes easily accessible from the delivery desk. Deep shelves give us, for the first time, a suitable place for bound newspapers, while certain alcoves have been fitted with deep drawers to hold our large and constantly growing collection of maps.

It is expected that this additional space for storing books will meet the needs of the Library for some years.

This generous gift from one of the College's most distinguished sons is, I believe, an evidence of the interest felt in the Library by the alumni of the College. Others have, by gifts of books and money, indicated their interest in and appreciation of the work which the Library is trying to do. Especially would I mention Mr. E. A. West, of Chicago, a member of the class of 1843, whose gifts, now extending over several years, have greatly assisted the Librarian in providing for some of the Library's most important needs, and have given him great encouragement. It is hoped that the interest of the alumni in the Library will be increased, and that they will feel free, by actual use or by correspondence, to avail themselves of its treasures.

Respectfully submitted,

AZARIAH S. ROOT.

REPORT OF THE DEPARTMENT OF MATHEMATICS.

To the Chairman of the Faculty :—

SIR: The number of freshmen studying mathematics is always so large, and the work with them requires so much careful attention, that it claims a large part of the time and strength of the teachers in this department.

Last year, with Professor Roe's efficient assistance, the work of the department was fully as strong as in any preceding year. The elective courses covered Advanced Analytic Geometry, the elements of the Differential and Integral Calculus, Advanced Integral Calculus, the Theory of Functions, and Surveying. In addition to my class-room work, I assisted a graduate student in a five-hour course of special work towards the degree of A. M.

The loss of Professor Roe has been a misfortune for the department. It has necessitated a considerable reduction in the courses offered, as Professor St. John can give only two thirds of his time to mathematics this year, and a still further reduction of the advanced work is proposed for next year.

During the present year Professor St. John and I have divided the freshman work equally. He also has a class meeting two hours per week in Mathematical Physics, and I have the regular sophomore work in the Calculus and a three-hour course in Analytic Mechanics.

Respectfully submitted,

F. ANDEREGG.

To the Chairman of the Faculty :—

SIR: In the department of Greek and Classical Archæology, during the past two years, there have been from sixty-five to seventy students in the required Greek of the Freshmen year, divided into two divisions.

The three-hour elective last year was devoted to Tragedy, and the same course this year is given to Comedy.   Between twenty-five and thirty students have elected this course.

In the two-hour elective last year a study was made of Greek Oratory; in the same course this year Historical and Philosophical Prose is studied. About twelve students are found in this course.

In Classical Archæology, the course in the History of Greek Sculpture was offered last year; this year the subject is a general one, the History of Ancient Art.   The Tuesday afternoon exercises which are held in Bradley Auditorium and illustrated by means of the stereopticon, are attended by a considerable number of students of whom attendance is not required.

The great need of the Department of Greek is more money for the library.   Respectfully submitted,

CHARLES B. MARTIN.

REPORT OF THE DEPARTMENT OF LATIN.

To the Chairman of the Faculty :—

SIR: I have taught during the two years two sections of elective Latin; reading Virgil's Georgics, with 33 students; three plays of Plautus, with 13 students; eleven orations of Cicero with 31 and 19 students; Catullus, with 37 students; Juvenal (six letters), with 13 students; Annals of Tacitus (four books), with 23 students; Lucretius (three books), with 6 students, and Livy, with 27 students.

Respectfully submitted,

L. B. HALL.

To the Chairman of the Faculty :—

SIR: The Freshman Latin was taught last year in four sections during the fall and winter terms; in three during the spring term.   The same plan is followed for the present year.   The authors read are Livy, Cicero, De Senectute and De Amicitia, Tacitus (Germania and Agricola), Horace (Odes and Epodes), and Terence.   The increase this year in the number taking Fresman Latin is shown by the enrollment of 145 pupils for the fall term as against 98 for the same period last year.   I have given a two-hour course in Roman History through the fall and winter terms, with an average attendance of 30.   The department greatly needs increased library facilities for the study of Roman history, institutions and private life.

Respectfully submitted,

C. K. CHASE.

14

REPORT OF THE DEPARTMENT OF THE GERMAN LANGUAGE AND LITERATURE.

To the Chairman of the Faculty :—

SIR: For the past two years the department has offered nineteen hours each term, eight of required and eleven of elective work. The number of students enrolled has been, per term, 181, 181, 151, for last year, and 200, 194, for the first two terms of the present year. There have been, besides each year, about twenty College students beginning German in the Academy. Last year two hours of the teaching was done by Professor Anderegg, two by Professor Wightman, and the remainder by myself. This year Professor Wightman is teaching two hours, and I am teaching seventeen. A club for German conversation, with an average membership of fifty, meets once a week.

It is the aim of the department so to conduct the work that the student who shall avail himself of all the courses offered may, during the four years, gain (1) a reading knowledge of ordinary German; (2) ability to pronounce and write simple German correctly, with some facility in speaking; (3) a critical knowledge of the chief masterpieces of German literature. The student who has had two years of German before entering College may hope to do more than this.

The limitations imposed upon the German work by the recent reduction of the teaching force, to which I referred in my last report, and which I would respectfully present to your attention again, while they do not, I believe, prevent very creditable work being done, are yet so serious that they should not be allowed to continue. As soon as the financial situation in any way admits, the College should have the full time of a second instructor in German.

Respectfully submitted,

ARLETTA M. ABBOTT.

REPORT OF THE DEPARTMENT OF ROMANCE LANGUAGES,

To the Chairman of the Faculty :—

SIR: Since the rendering of the last report, two years ago, the work in this department has remained substantially the same.

Fourteen hours of French have been taught each year in college, viz.: 1, A five-hour course for beginners; 2, 3 and 4, a five-hour course for students entering college with two terms of preparation, divided into (1) a two-hour course in Reading, (2) a two-hour course in Grammar and Conversation, and (3) a one-hour course in Composition; 5, a two-hour course in

French Prose Writers, especially intended for students who enter college with two years of preparation in French; and two elective courses, viz., 6, one of two hours in French Poetry ('96 and '97), or in French Drama ('97 and '98); and 7, a course of one hour in advanced French Composition. Of these courses Mr. Cowdery has taught Nos. 2 and 4.

A three-term course of two hours weekly has also been taught each year in Italian.

In addition to the work in his own department, your professor has in both years taught a two hour elective in German. He regrets the necessity for this, as it has reduced the already small number of advanced electives in French.

The French Club has continued to hold weekly meetings, and has proved a valuable supplement in various ways to the work of the class-room.

We have been glad to welcome from time to time considerable additions to the list of books in the library upon French and Italian literature.

Respectfully submitted,

J. R. WIGHTMAN.

REPORT OF THE DEPARTMENT OF CHEMISTRY AND MINERALOGY.

To the Chairman of the Faculty :—

SIR: No important changes have been introduced in the methods of carrying on the work of the Chemical Department since the last report.

In Elementary Chemistry, instruction has been given partly by the use of a good text book and partly by lectures, the latter mainly on the fundamental principles of the science and on the more recent discoveries; the former, when the general descriptive matter pertaining to the subject was involved.

The number of students in the class has far exceeded the seating capacity of the lecture room, necessitating two divisions and the repetition of the lecture.

The work of the class-room has been supplemented by the no less important laboratory work, and although the latter is not required, eighty-five per cent. of the students in Chemistry labored enthusiastically and with good success in the laboratory. All laboratory expenses are covered by an extra fee.

The subject of Qualitative Chemical Analysis is studied mainly in the laboratory, although lectures are frequently given. When properly pursued, this subject is of great value in the development of the reasoning powers, by the application of the knowledge gained, by the careful study of phenomena observed in bringing about chemical reactions, and in using these reactions for the separation of compounds from one another.

The classes in Quantitative Analysis and in Organic Chemistry last spring were unusually large, and the work done very satisfactory.

Instruction in Mineralogy is given both by lectures, treating of Crystallography and Descriptive Mineralogy, and by practical work in the laboratory. For the study of Crystallography, the department is well supplied with a large collection of wooden models, and a smaller collection of natural crystals.

During the past year the mineral collection has been enlarged and greatly enriched by the addition of minerals valued at a thousand dollars, in part secured by purchase, and in part the gift of Rev. R. T. Cross, of York, Neb.

Respectfully submitted,

F. F. JEWETT.

REPORT OF THE DEPARTMENT OF PHYSICS AND ASTRONOMY.

To the Chairman of the Faculty :—

SIR: The short time that has passed since the Department of Physics and Astronomy was placed in charge of the present head of the department, and the fact that two-thirds of the time of the department during this year has been given to assisting in the Department of Mathematics, renders unnecessary the presenting of an extended report.

Two sections of freshman mathematics and a two-hour cou rse of mor advanced mathematical work — the application of some mathematical principles to a few definite physical problems in vibratory motion with special reference to their importance in sound, light and electricity — have been in charge of this department. Owing to these circumstances the course in Astronomy has been omitted this year. This temporary suspension of the course was rendered the less objectionable because Astronomy was given twice last year by Professor Churchill to large classes.

A five-hour course in Physics has been given, which extends through the year. This consists of three hours of lecture and recitation work and two laboratory periods per week. The work of the first term covers an introduction to Mechanics and the Theory of Sound, with particular reference to the relation between sound and music; Light and Heat occupy the second term, and the third term is given to Electricity and Magnetism. These are in no sense technical courses, but aim to supply that training and that knowledge of the several parts of the subject that may well form a part of a liberal education. A physical laboratory is now open to the students in Physics. The plan this year is to begin the equipment of a laboratory for the first year of College Physics; and by far the major part of the funds available for this department have heen expended for this purpose. The aim is to equip the laboratory with apparatus of the same grade as is used in " Physics C " in Harvard College, and to give substantially the same or an equivalent laboratory course. The work in the laboratory runs parallel with the text book and lecture work. The present appropriation has been expended more for extended sets of apparatus than for expensive single pieces, and only for such sets of apparatus as are now considered standard things for this grade of work. The main single items of expenditure are for the heavy oak laboratorv tables, a spectrometer, Sabine's form; a Rowland D'Arsonval galvanometer, and an ampere-volt meter. The department rejoices also in a new lecture table of solid oak, supplied with water, gas and electric connections, which adds greatly to the convenience and efficiency of the lecture work.

The lines along which it is hoped future development may take place are indicated in the following brief statement of the aims and plans of the department: The laboratory method of teaching Physics demands an equipment quite distinct from the demonstration apparatus used for illustrative purposes in the lecture room. The latter is on the whole mainly qualitative, or but roughly quantitative, in its results, while no work that is not rigidly quantitative in character can hold high rank as College laboratory work in Physics; measurement — accurate measurement — is the only solid basis for the work.

Physical problems, involving laws elaborated in the lectures and susceptible of definite numerical results, are set for thc student, and he can be held as strictly responsible as when he is given exercises in mathematics; his powers of observation are increased and rendered accurate; but of far greater value, for intellectual brains, is the exercise of the judgment in the discussion of the results and in the consideration of means to reduce the effect of accidental and unavoidable errors to a minimum; but perhaps the highest value must be put upon the increased ability of the student to see the facts with an unbiased mind and to record them conscientiously. This last result is mainly rendered possible by the fact that the final outcome of a long and more or less varied series of measurements is to be brought to a numerical test by deducing, by means of established formulæ, the required conclusions, and the foreknowledge on the part of the student does not permit him to say just what values the individual measurements ought to have, so that in taking these observations he is thrown entirely upon his own conscientious and painstaking effort.

The equipment of a physical laboratory that will assist in doing these

, is the immediate aim of this department. Following
ral Physics, other and more advanced courses will be
ient of the department permits and circumstances de-
the advanced courses will be to permit students pos-
tude in these lines to pursue the subject further, and to
ies for more extended preparation to those who expect to
teach the ᴗᴗ ; and the needs of those students will be considered who
plan to enter upon a technical or engineering course after leaving Oberlin.
This does not contemplate the giving of technical laboratory work, but in
nearly all such courses a sound and thorough preparation along physical
lines is obtained during the first two years; and as graduates of Oberlin will
enter upon such courses with advanced standing, it is very desirable that
they shall not be placed at a disadvantage by lack of the earlier work which
must precede the purely technical application in the later years of their
technical courses.

The most pressing need of the department which is now unprovided
for is that of increased library facilities, both for the current literature of
the subject and for general works of reference. Of the latter, there is almost a total lack in the College library.

Respectfully submitted,
CHARLES EDWARD ST. JOHN.

REPORT OF THE DEPARTMENT OF BOTANY.

To the Chairman of the Faculty :—

SIR: Few changes have been made in the work of the department.
The course in Systematic Botany offered in the winter term has been
dropped, and a course in Vegetable Physiology substituted. At present
work in Systematic Botany can be elected during any term. The herbarium
continues to grow rapidly in size and efficiency. On his retirement, Professor Kelsey presented his large and valuable collection to the College. It
is largely due to interest shown by Professor Kelsey that the herbarium has
grown to its present size. The number of specimens is now several times
greater than it was at the time of the appointment of Professor Kelsey. It
is estimated that about 7,000 specimens have been added during the present
year. These are as follows: Five hundred species collected in the vicinity
of Washington by Mr. E. S. Steele, an alumnus of Oberlin. These were
named by experts in the Department of Agriculture. Mr. Steele has at
various times presented to the herbarium several thousand specimens. In
addition to the above there are 500 from Japan, 1,500 from New England,
1,000 from Ohio, 263 from Oklahoma, 165 from New Mexico, 300 from Kan-

sas, 200 from Wyoming, and 2,500 from other sources. The
now contains nearly 35,000 specimens, representing 13,000 or 14,000 s

The danger from fire in the present building is very great, and we
only hope that the time is not far distant when the herbarium can be moved
to a fireproof building. The Botany Club has met regularly once in two
weeks, the attendance averaging between twenty and thirty. The aim during the present year has been to have presented to the Club papers dealing
with the recent advances in botany.

The principal needs of the department are suitable charts for the
illustration of lectures, apparatus costing approximately $300 for laboratory
work in Physiology, one or more greenhouses for experimental purposes and
the raising of plants needed for illustration and class use.

It is not the policy of the department to expand the work much, if any,
beyond the present limits, but to increase as much as possible the efficiency
of the courses already offered.

Respectfully submitted,

HERBERT L. JONES.

REPORT OF THE DEPARTMENT OF GEOLOGY AND ZOOLOGY.

To the Chairman of the Faculty :—

SIR: There have been no changes in the arrangement of the courses in
this department since the last report. The general work for the College
which has been imposed upon the professor has necessitated that the laboratory work of the department should be thrown very largely upon the assistant, Mr. Lynds Jones. We are fortunate in having one in the service of
the College who is so well able to carry this work, and the classes have
been prosperous under the arrangement.

Mr. Jones has also taught a number of classes independently, in Anatomy and Ornithology, and it is not too much to say that a very general interest in the latter subject, of a thoroughly scientific kind, has been aroused
in the College and the town. He has also been the principal dependence of
the Zoological Club.

THE MUSEUM.

All attempts at an adequate exhibition of our excellent museum material have had to be abandoned, as nearly all the space in the former museum
room in the Library building has been given up for library and laboratory
needs. Some of the cases have been removed to other buildings; the remainder have been piled, one above the other, regardless of lighting or convenience of access, while the contents of many others have been boxed up

and stowed away in the cellar. A limited series for use in lectures is still available, and much labor is expended upon the rest to preserve it from destruction. However, considerable systematic work has been done in elaborating new material, and collections of value are constantly being made.

Respectfully submitted,

ALBERT A. WRIGHT.

REPORT OF THE DEPARTMENT OF ENGLISH AND AMERICAN HISTORY.

To the Chairman of the Faculty :—

SIR: During the year '96-'97 I taught one class in Elementary English History with 35, 34 and 21 students; a class in elementary American History with 28, 33 and 16 students; and a class in advanced American History with 4, 4 and 5 students. During the year '97-'98 I have repeated these courses with 28 and 28, 26 and 27, 4 and 2 students. I have also added an advanced course in English History with 6 students each term. These advanced courses I have managed much like university seminaries, and the results in interest and in thoroughness have been very gratifying to the teacher.

Respectfully submitted,

L. B. HALL.

REPORT OF THE DEPARTMENT OF RHETORIC AND ORATORY.

To the Chairman of the Faculty :—

SIR: Since the last report of the Department of Rhetoric and Oratory the courses have been rearranged for the purpose of giving a larger freedom for electives. Heretofore English Composition has been required for one term of the freshman, sophomore and junior classes. The junior course has now been transferred to the sophomore year, leaving the junior and senior years open for elective work. The elective courses are two, one in Oratorical Composition, which has to do with the Expository Address, the Argumentative Address, and the Extemporaneous Debate; the other — conducted in part by Professor Cressy — has to do with a more distinctively literary form of composition. Both courses run throughout the year, so that it is possible for the student to do advanced work in composition during the junior and senior years.

The work, however, has grown beyond our facilities. The College budget appropriates but eight hundred dollars for the department, and only two-thirds of the professor's time can be devoted to the work. The other third is devoted to the elocution work in the Theological Seminary; whereas, when the time needed to correct compositions is added to regular work of the class-room, the total amount is more than one man could do if he had his entire time for the work. We have an instructor in Elocution and English Composition, but no appropriation is made for his salary. In order to pay his salary, it has been necessary to charge a fee for all the work in elocution, and to put that fee so high that the elocution work might pay not only for itself, but for much of the composition work as well. This is very unfortunate, for it places the work in elocution beyond the reach of most College students. The department is seriously handicapped by having to work upon so meager an appropriation as eight hundred dollars.

Respectfully submitted,

FRED M. TISDEL.

REPORT OF THE DEPARTMENT OF ENGLISH.

To the Chairman of the Faculty :—

SIR: During the past year (including last Spring term, last Fall term, and the present Winter term) the following courses have been given in English Language and Literature: English 4, Anglo Saxon (elected by 20 students); English 5, Early Middle English (elected by 19 students); English 6, Chaucer (elected by 14 students); English 7, Shakespeare (elected by 73 students); English 8, Shakespeare (elected by 53 students); English 9, Shakespeare (elected by 30 students); English 12, Milton (elected by 13 students); English 13, Poets of the Eighteenth and Nineteenth Centuries (elected by 43 students); English 14, Prose Writers of the Eighteenth and Nineteenth Centuries (elected by 34 students). The courses in Modern Literature have been elected about as usual. The number electing Shakespeare has slightly increased. The largest increase in election has occurred in the courses in Anglo Saxon, Early Middle English and Chaucer, which courses, taken together, form a continuous study in the development of the English language. The class in this work, meeting five times a week, remains practically the same throughout the year. The collegiate age of this class becomes a little younger year by year, as students who wish to make the major study of their course English are realizing that they should get their foundation in Old English laid, if possible, as early as their sophomore year. The department is much hampered by an insufficient library; but has recently been fortunate in receiving much help from valuable books added to the library of the Union Library Association.

Respectfully submitted,

WILFRED W. CRESSY.

REPORT OF THE DEPARTMENT OF ECONOMICS AND SOCIOLOGY.

To the Chairman of the Faculty :—

SIR: During the spring term of 1896 the regular introductory course in Political Economy was given, and the course in Money and Banking, which had been given the previous fall, was repeated at the request of a number of students, the course on Socialism being dropped to make room for it. In addition, courses on Economic Problems, on the Theory of the State, and the Economic Seminar were carried.

Beginning with the fall term of 1896, the work in Economics was arranged with a number of alternating courses, so that for the last two years the following cycle has been, or is being, carried out:

1896-7—
1. Advanced Economic Theory, three hours. Fall and winter.
2. Distribution of Wealth, two hours. Fall.
3. History of Political Economy, two hours. Winter.
4. Introductory course in Political Economy, five hours. Spring.
5. Economic Problems, two hours. Throughout the year.
6. Economic Seminar. Throughout the year.

1897-8—
1. Money and Banking, three hours. Fall.
2. Finance and Taxation, three hours. Winter.
3. Transportation, two hours. Fall.
4. Industrial History, two hours. Winter.
5. Introductory course in Political Economy, five hours. Spring.
6. Economic Seminar. Throughout the year.

It is the opinion of the instructor that the introductory course in Political Economy should be changed to the fall, when it might be elected by juniors, instead of in the spring term of the sophomore year as at present. He is also in doubt as to the advisability of carrying so many short courses; otherwise he is satisfied with the present arrangement.

The courses in Sociology have been arranged with those in Political Science in a two-year cycle, as follows:

1896-7—
1. Anthropology, three hours. Fall.
2. Principles of Sociology, three hours. Winter.
3. Practical Sociology, three hours. Spring.

1897-8—
1. Elementary Law, three hours. Fall.
2. American Constitutional Law, three hours. Winter.
3. International Law, three hours. Spring.
4. Comparative Politics. Throughout the year.

By this arrangement a larger number of electives can be offered, and it makes it possible to carry on some of the work formerly given by Professor Monroe. The disadvantages are that it spreads the work of a single instructor over a wide field. This is especially felt in the courses in Political Science, but it does not seem advisable to drop such courses out of the College curriculum.

The interest in the work of the department seems encouraging, and some excellent work has been done by individual students — work which has received flattering recognition in larger universities and in economic publications.

Respectfully submitted,

T. N. CARVER.

REPORT OF THE DEPARTMENT OF PSYCHOLOGY AND PEDAGOGY.

To the Chairman of the Faculty :—

SIR: The work of the year may be presented most conveniently under the heads of General Philosophy and Pedagogy.

I. *General Philosophy—Fall Term.*—a. Epistemology. Five hours. Elective. The development of the theory of knowledge, as contained in the writings of Locke, Berkeley and Hume, was studied critically.

b. Psychology. Five hours. Required. As introductory, the work was necessarily of a general character, treating of mental processes in their fundamental features rather than in a special way. The texts used (Wundt and James) insured that the student would be brought into contact with the latest methods and results.

Winter Term.—a. Epistemology. The course begun in the fall was continued. Students, having been familiarized with the field, were brought into close touch with the deeper problems of later modern thought through the study of Kant's Critique of Pure Reason.

b. Ethics. Mental processes were studied, not simply from the side of their structure (Psychology), but also from the side of their worth. Students were familiarized with the facts bearing upon the determination of the nature, history and justification of the moral ideal in its relation to personal life and action.

Spring Term.—a. Introduction to Philosophy. Five hours. Elective. The course served as a general introduction to philosophical investigation by way of the selected dialogues of Plato, and by means of the exposition of the various philosophical disciplines.

b. Experimental Psychology. Five hours. Elective. The purpose of the course was to familiarize the student with the methods and results of

24

later psychology, as it has endeavored to analyze mental processes by means of careful and exact experiments upon the physical organism.

II. *Pedagogy.*—A continuous course, running throughout the year, was offered. In the fall term the students were familiarized with the facts of previous systems of education as these were seen on the background of the general life of the time. In the winter term investigation was made of the bearing of psychology and ethics upon the actual process of education, while in the spring term the results reached were systematized in a course of lectures dealing with the more fundamental questions which concern the general nature of education.

Respectfully submitted,

S. F. MacLennan.

REPORT OF THE PROFESSOR OF PHYSIOLOGY AND DIRECTOR OF THE MEN'S GYMNASIUM.

To the Chairman of the Faculty :—

SIR: Few changes have been made in the work of this department during the two years which have elapsed since the last report. The following courses are now offered each year: College electives—Human Physiology (five hours per week), Personal and Public Hygiene (two hours); to second years in the Normal Course in Physical Training for Women—Literature of Physical Training 1 (three hours) and 2 (two hours), History of Physical Training (one hour); to first years in the Normal Course and to students preparing to teach in the Men's Gymnasium—Physiology of Exercise (two hours), and Gymnastic Theory (two hours). The courses given in the fall term are: Gymnastic Theory, and Literature of Physical Training 1; in the winter, Human Physiology, and Literature of Physical Training 2; in the spring, Hygiene, Physiology of Exercise, and History of Physical Training. A five-hour course in Human Anatomy is being given this term in response to a request from five young men who are planning to study medicine. A number of medical schools in which the course of study extends over four years will admit to the second year students who have completed in a recognized college a certain amount of work in chemistry, physics, biology, and related sciences, and the addition of the course in anatomy makes it possible for our graduates to meet this requirement, at least in the case of some schools. The course is a partial one, including the study of bones, joints and muscles, and can be profitably taught with the illustrative material at hand. It is not the intention to offer it regularly, but only as occeason arises.

The physical examination of new students in the Academy and College occupies a large part of my time in the fall term, until the middle of November, and then the gymnasium is opened for the year. No work is done indoors after the first weeks in May, but from that time until Commencement second examinations are made for all students who request them. The gymnasium office is open for a half hour on five days of the week during the entire year. In addition to this, I am in the Registrar's office one hour on Mondays, and one hour on other days is regularly set apart for the convenience of students who wish to talk over their physical condition or confer concerning matters of personal hygiene. Last year the editing of the College catalogue was added to other duties in the spring, and the same task has been assigned for the present year.

No alterations have been made in the gymnasium beyond the introduction of incandescent lights, eight in the main room and two in the dressing room. This very agreeable change from oil lamps was made possible by the teachers in the gymnasium, who donated for the purpose a part of the proceeds of a gymnastic entertainment prepared and given by them for the benefit of the Athletic Association. The running expense of these lights is met by a small fee charged for the use of lockers. Last fall the Prudential Committee authorized an expenditure for preliminary plans of a new men's gymnasium, and sketches and specifications have accordingly been sent to the firm of Chicago architects engaged for the work. These plans will serve to express the wishes of the department, and they will also furnish a center about which criticisms and further suggestions may crystallize.

The successful working of the department depends so largely upon the efficiency of the students employed to teach classes in the gymnasium (after they have received at least a year of special preparation, as explained in the report of 1895), that the names of those who serve the College in this capacity are deserving of record. The teachers who graduated last June were W. C. Clancy, C. K. Fauver, J. H. McMurray and H. A. Young. Those at present engaged are R. L. Cheney, J. M. Davis, W. B. Elmore, Edgar and Edwin Fauver, J. F. Rudolph, W. F. Thatcher and A. Winter. Their interest and faithful co-operation have been a constant source of encouragement in the face of an inadequate equipment, which frequently suggests the historical attempt at making "bricks without straw."

The summer of 1896 was spent upon the continent of Europe, and chiefly in Germany. The visit gave opportunity to gain some familiarity with the rich German literature of physical training, and to see a number of typical indoor and open-air gymnasia, together with illustrations of German popular and educational gymnastics. The books and pamphlets secured, many of them to be obtained only by personal search, are not the least valuable trophies of what was at the same time a most restful vacation. Last May the North American (German) Gymnastic Union held its quadrennial gymnastic festival in St. Louis. Through the courtesy of the National Executive Committee I was invited to serve on the special Committee of Observation, and for three days, as the guest of the Union, was given every opportunity to see to the best advantage the largest and most interesting gymnastic gathering to be witnessed in our country. At the meeting of the National Educational Association in Milwaukee last July a paper on "Physical Training in the Colleges" was read before the Physical Education Department.

Respectfully submitted,

FRED EUGENE LEONARD.

REPORT OF THE DIRECTOR OF THE WOMAN'S GYMNASIUM.

To the Chairman of the Faculty:—

SIR: The general plan of the work of the Woman's Gymnasium has not been changed since the last report. During the director's absence of two terms her work was efficiently carried on by Dr. Elizabeth Newcomb. The enrollment for the year 1896-7 was 375, and so far during the current year it has been 372. The entire enrollment since 1885, as represented by the number of physical examinations made, is 2,788.

In addition to the usual reports for Gymnasium attendance, where for two-thirds of the number the work is compulsory, a record is now being kept of the number of hours each young woman spends in the open air. The lowest average is one and eight-tenths hours per week, the highest twelve and two-tenths hours; the general average, six and one-third hours. Although the general average equals the number of hours required in many schools where out-of-door exercise is compulsory, still it is insufficient. This and the uneven distribution among individuals make it advisable that more attention be paid to out-of-door sports in the future.

Something has already been done along this line. In the spring of 1897 one out-of-door basket ball court was enclosed and laid out, and the following class teams organized: Junior, Sophomore, Freshman, Physical Training, Senior Academy, and Mixed Academy. Team practice was popular, and eleven class games were enthusiastically played. The courts on the skating-floor are still used on rainy days and for beginning classes, but a hardwood floor is a dangerous place to play matched games.

A Young Woman's Tennis Association was formed the same spring, and the two courts belonging to the Gymasium placed under its management. One court was put in good order by the Association and used for playing the games of the tournament. Bicycle and skating lessons have been given on the skating-floor, a small fee being charged. Plans for other forms of out-door exercise are in progress and will be put in execution during the spring term. Although more attention is being paid to out-door exercise and games, the in-door work is receiving the same careful attention as heretofore.

Miss Cory, the assistant, spent the summer of 1896 in scientific study at the University of Wisconsin, and in November of the same year represented the Woman's Gymnasium at the meeting of the Ohio Physical Education Association held in Cincinnati. The director spent a month of the summer of 1897 doing special work in lateral curvature and weak foot with Dr. L. A. Weigel, of Rochester.

Bryn Mawr College has been furnished during the past two years with six hundred anthropometric charts for recording measurements. The chart used was the one compiled here in 895.

We note with gratification that the young women are coming more and more to recognize physical training as a valuable part of their education, and to plan as definitely for it as they do for their literary work.

NORMAL COURSE IN PHYSICAL TRAINING.

Most of the progress made in this department has been in developing the work along lines previously laid down.

The following changes have been made: Zoology, since the term of work on "The Gross Anatomy of the Cat" has been added to the course, has not seemed so necessary as a preparation for human physiology, and it has been dropped. In Human Anatomy two hours have been added, making a seven-hour course. Dr. Miriam T. Runyon is now teaching this course. Excellent preparation and previous experience in that line of work enables her to present the subject in a thorough and practical manner.

In the spring of 1897 Miss Sigrid Ruth, a graduate of Central Institute, Stockholm, gave four lectures on Medical Gymnastics to the second year class. Dr. Karl Zapp, of Cleveland, is again giving the Physical Training Club a series of lessons on fencing.

The usual number of grades in the public schools have been taught by the students of the Normal Course. In addition to this, twenty-four lessons have been given to the Kindergarten teachers. The work was planned by the director, but the instruction was given by Miss N. E. Leyde, a graduate of the Normal Course.

The following additions have been made to the equipment: Forty-two dollars have been spent on the reference library. Twenty-five new books have been purchased and a number of pamphlets bound. A beginning has been made toward furnishing the skating floor with apparatus; Swedish climbing ropes, vaulting box and ladder have been placed there, costing $76.10. These give added facilities for exercise, not only to the young women of the Normal Course, but to the young women of the college also.

28

A small room is being fitted up for giving practical instruction in massage and medical gymnastics. The present need of the department is for anatomical models for class-room demonstration.

There is a noticeable improvement in the previous preparation of the students who enter this course. The number enrolled for the year 1896–7 was thirteen, and is the same for the current year. Six young women were graduated at the last commencement.

Respectfully submitted,

DELPHINE HANNA.

REPORT OF THE DEPARTMENT OF DRAWING AND PAINTING.

To the Chairman of the Faculty:—

SIR: In making my fourth annual report, I am glad to record a steady increase in the number of students of this department. The number of pupils the first year of my teaching was 53. The number for the present year will probably reach 90, taking the number enrolled up to the present time as a basis. Another term of elective drawing has been added to the one already offered. Last year twenty-five students in college elected the first term of drawing, and seven the second term, making in all thirty-four terms against three terms of the first year. The extra tuition for this work precludes any but a serious purpose in electing the course, and it is very encouraging that the number is so large.

For the present year instruction in object drawing is given the members of the Kindergarten Training School outside the regular teaching hours. In addition to the weekly sketch class, an evening class has been formed for the more advanced pupils. The College Annual proves a real incentive to good work, and the drawings of students representing this department are improving in quality and number each year. Our most urgent need is a larger number of casts.

Respectfully submitted,

EVA M. OAKES.

REPORT OF THE WOMAN'S DEPARTMENT.

To the Chairman of the Faculty:—

SIR: The enrollment for the spring term was 565, for the fall term 655, for the winter term 658. These figures, contrasted with those of the last current year, show a loss in the spring term of 35, but a gain in the fall term of 41, and in the winter term of 33.

There has been no prevailing sickness during the year. Our greatest danger in this climate is from colds, and from this cause we suffer every winter. Some success has attended Dr. Hanna's efforts to teach the women of the College how to live and avoid this evil.

A careful observer for the last few years could hardly fail to note a marked improvement in our order. This is partly due, no doubt, to the fact that society in general is better organized. Our young women, as a rule, come from refined homes, and are a law unto themselves. But it should not be forgotten, in this connection, that the Woman's Department is so organized that it is not attractive to the lawless woman or to the fortune hunter. When such appear in our midst, a little patience is all that is necessary; for when they find they must be in their rooms every evening at an early hour — that they cannot be absent from their boarding places for any great length of time without permission — they quietly pack their trunks and go away. Since the opening of the College in September there has not been a case of discipline serious enough to necessitate its being referred to the Woman's Board.

Time only emphasizes the wisdom of our boarding arrangements. Our various halls have been most successfully managed this year. Keep Home, Stewart Hall, Talcott Hall, Baldwin Cottage and Lord Cottage have each an ideal matron, and I doubt if for the money paid more comfortable homes can be found. For those who do not enjoy large families there is the relief of private homes, of which we have more than seventy-five. Oberlin owes a debt of gratitude to the matrons of these homes, who so heartily sympathize with the College and work so earnestly for the highest good of our young people.

Respectfully submitted,

A. A. F. JOHNSTON, Dean.

GENERAL REPORT OF THE THEOLOGICAL SEMINARY.

To the Chairman of the Faculty :—

SIR: A considerable number of changes that would not naturally appear in the reports of individual professors have occurred in the Seminary, and it has been thought best to present them in a general report. The individual reports reveal the fact that the curriculum has been improved by the addition of a number of new courses. Professor King's course in Microcosmus has been included in the theological curriculum. Courses in Encyclopedia, Sociology, Missions, an English Bible course in the Old Testament and in the New Testament, a New Testament Seminar and a Seminar in History of Doctrine have been added.

In some cases these courses have displaced or are modifications of other courses, but in the main they are additions to the curriculum. The logical relations of the different parts of the curriculum have been somewhat emphasized by fixing upon a required order in which certain studies must be taken. The course in Encyclopedia, which outlines the theological course and shows the mutual relationship of the various departments of theological study, is open only to Juniors. Students are now recommended, though not required, to begin their Church History in the Junior year, which leaves them two years in which to pursue the various Church History electives based upon this general course in the external history of the church. These changes are not such as to prevent a due amount of specialization, which our extensive elective system was devised to secure.

The number of hours required for graduation has been increased to 1440; that is, 15 hours per week of attendance upon lectures for three years. Upon the completion of this course those that are college graduates receive, as heretofore, the degree of D. B. In the case of such as are not college graduates, the requirement for admission to the classical course, and for the attainment of the degree D. B. upon its completion, have been somewhat increased. The requirement for admission in such cases is preparation for the college classical course, and in addition the following studies: Logic or History of Philosophy, Psychology, Ethics, General History (preferably that of the Roman Empire and the Middle Ages), Rhetoric, two courses in English Literature, Political Economy, and two Natural Sciences. Some work in English in the Gospels, including a chronology of the life of Christ, work in the Historical Books of the English Old Testament, and a reading knowledge of German are recommended as desirable. Those who are not college graduates are to receive, upon completion of the three-year course, a diploma constituting them alumni of the Seminary, but not conferring upon them the degree D. B. They may, however, if their work during the three years has been satisfactory, be permitted by vote of the faculty to receive the degree after a fourth year of work selected from the electives of the Seminary and College, at least two-thirds of the work to consist of Seminary electives; or in rare cases of exceptionally high scholarship, non-college graduates may receive the degree at the end of the third year.

It is becoming more and more evident that in the Seminary, as in other professional schools, there must be a four instead of a three-year curriculum, so arranged that the studies of the first year may be included among those of the Junior and Senior years of the College course. We have, therefore, in our new catalogue, published a recommended four-year course, showing to college students preparing for the ministry what theological studies they ought to take while in college, and how they may best arrange the work of the three years after graduation from college. We have specified Philosophy of Religion (e. g., Microcosmus), Hebrew, Christian Evidences, Sociology, History — particularly History of the Roman Empire, Middle Ages, and of England — as studies that might be taken in college and constitute the first year of such a four-year course.

We have recommended to the Trustees that the English course be discontinued in view of the difficulty of securing its financial support. This recommendation is made after strenuous and prolonged effort to raise the money required to carry on the course. In spite of such effort, by the end of the present year the College Treasurer will have advanced a sum probably not far from $1,200. It has been ascertained that the work of the Slavic Department can be carried on without the English Department, although many of the Slavic students have been taught in classes of the English Department. In has been arranged, also, in case the English Department be given up, to receive as special students a limited number of such as are already ordained ministers and have done successful work in the ministry, but who are not able to meet the requirements for admission into the Classical Course. For these students two or three years of work can be arranged in such of the regular courses as they would be able to take with profit. It has been felt that the Seminary should hold itself in readiness to do what it can, in the way just described, to raise the standard of education among such inadequately educated men as may be already in the service of the churches.

During the coming year an experiment is to be made in the appropriation of beneficiary aid. Any student who is taking fewer than twelve hours of lectures per week, or who does not attain a standing of 75 per cent. in his work, will be required to take the aid he may need as a loan instead of a gift. Furthermore, the five applicants for beneficiary aid who attain the highest standing in their classes, provided that standing be above a certain limit, are to receive an extra appropriation. The usual amount of aid given by the Education Society and from our own funds, which is between $125 and $150, will be increased in one case to $200, in two cases to $175, and in two other cases to $150.

The attendance the present year is not quite as large as last year, which is perhaps due to the fact that we graduated last year a class of twenty-two members, a larger class than we usually receive, and to the fact that in general fewer men have entered upon theological study the present year.

Signed by A. H. CURRIER, Chairman.
E. I. BOSWORTH, Secretary.

REPORT OF THE DEPARTMENT OF OLD TESTAMENT LANGUAGE AND LITERATURE.

To the Chairman of the Faculty :—

SIR: The work of this department has not been materially changed since the last report. It stands at present as follows: Hebrew for beginners, five hours through the year. Four two-hour courses are offered in Advanced Hebrew, each for one semester. Hebrew is elective. All students are required to take a two-hour course in Old Testament Introduction, chiefly analysis of all the books; it is proposed to make this course three hours per week. Non-Hebrew students are required to do work in the English Old Testament, work that is open to all, viz., a course in Outlines of Old Testament Theology, and one in Messianic Prophecy. It is proposed to lengthen these from two to three hours.

Last fall a course was offered in English Exegesis of Job. While it proved a profitable course, it seems scarcely advisable to continue to offer such a course, lest it prevent proper attention to Hebrew exegesis.

Respectfully submitted,

OWEN H. GATES.

REPORT OF THE DEPARTMENT OF NEW TESTAMENT LANGUAGE AND LITERATURE.

To the Chairman of the Faculty :—

SIR: The work in this department has gone on regularly since the last report. All the courses have been given, and the work of the students, upon the whole, has been exceedingly well done.

There will be added next year a New Testament seminar, the general subject of which for some time to come will be the Jewish background of the Gospels. This is intended to include not merely the political and social environment of the Gospel narrative, but also the religious conceptions prevalent among the Jews in the time of Jesus.

The two-hour course in Special New Testament Introduction, given last year for the first time, will be a three-hour course next year. The aim of this course is to go over in English such books of the New Testament as are not studied in Greek during any given two years, so that the students in this department during their course may acquire some degree of familiarity with the whole New Testament. These books are not treated solely from the standpoint of introduction, but an effort is made also to get the principal exegetical problems of each book before the class, and to put them in such shape that they can be readily taken up by the men after leaving the Seminary.

I hope by this means, in connection with another device, soon to be in a position to direct the New Testament study of any who may wish it, for some years after they graduate. For several years, by the use of duplicating apparatus, I have supplied each member of the class with a full list of questions upon each lesson, from the replies to which he constructs his own commentary upon the book under discussion. At the same time, complete copies of my own lectures have been provided for each student, thus saving for reports and discussions the time of the class hour that otherwise would have been used in dictation. It is my plan to take up some new work each year, and by sending through the mail these questions and copies of my own lectures, to keep any recent graduates that may desire it in touch with the work being done here.

There has also been added a two-hour course in English Bible Exegesis to be given every second year.

Since the subjects of the elective courses are constantly rotating, it is now possible for a student during three years to take 274 hours of Greek Exegesis, which is equivalent to $8\frac{1}{2}$ hours per week for one year; 56 hours of Biblical Theology of the New Testament; 54 hours of Special Introduction; 36 hours of English Bible Exegesis. Regarding the Biblical Theology as work in the English Bible, there are thus given during the course 146 hours of English Bible, which is equivalent to $4\frac{1}{2}$ hours per week for one year. This seems to meet, partially, at least, the demand for English Bible which is being made upon the Seminaries, without detriment to the Greek work. There are also given 32 hours of General Introduction and 56 hours of Seminar. To keep this amount of work going requires on my part ten hours of teaching per week.

The chief need of the department is that which has been regularly stated in these reports, hitherto without result, namely, money for books to be added to the Library.

Respectfully submitted,

EDWARD I. BOSWORTH.

REPORT OF THE DEPARTMENT OF CHURCH HISTORY.

To the Chairman of the Faculty :—

SIR: The Department of Church History has one or two changes of a superficial nature to report. The General Church History, being largely an introductory course, is now given in the junior year. The History of Doctrine, instead of running through two years as a two-hour elective, is now given every year as a three-hour required study for the middle class, so that it may precede the Theology, which is to be a senior study. A seminar elective in connection with the History of Doctrine will enable students who desire it to obtain a more thorough knowledge of important phases of the subject. The elective work given this year in addition to the above has been a course on the Development of Religious Liberty and Toleration, and one on the History of the American Church. Twenty-four persons have been connected with my courses during the year.

I may say that it has been with a great sense of relief that I have been permitted to give my individual time this year to the work of my department, which grows in importance and should grow in efficiency with every year. Respectfully submitted,

ALBERT T. SWING.

REPORT OF THE DEPARTMENT OF HOMILETICS AND PRACTICAL THEOLOGY.

To the Chairman of the Faculty :—

SIR: In my report of the work in my department of instruction in Oberlin Theological Seminary for this year, I have but few changes in the usual course of study to speak of. It remains substantially the same as reported in my last account of it.

My aim in my Homiletic instruction is to teach the students of my classes how to make themselves effective and successful preachers of the gospel. To this end, they are carefully trained in the use of those principles of sermon-making which long experience has approved. Special emphasis is laid upon the importance of making the sermon simple in language, clear in arrangement, scriptural in doctrine, inspiring in thought, and stimulating to right action and conduct. To give the young men greater facility in preparing themselves to preach, an extra course in Plan Construction has been given to them this year.

In Pastoral Theology, my instruction has been directed to such topics as are fitted to make my pupils intelligent in the subjects relating to the pastoral office, and efficient in the performance of its duties. To this end, I have added, this year, to my regular course of instruction in this branch of study an elective course in Sociology, in which I have discussed at considerable length, with sufficient fullness, I think, the principal social problems of the day, in the endeavor to show what, in our application of the teachings of Christianity to the needs of the times, may be wisely attempted, as proved by experience, to diminish the prevalence of crime, the miseries of poverty, and the discontent of the working classes.

Respectfully submitted,

A. H. CURRIER.

REPORT OF THE DEPARTMENT OF THE HARMONY OF SCIENCE AND REVELATION.

To the Chairman of the Faculty :—

SIR: The classes coming under my care during the past two years have been considerably larger than during the previous years. Those electing Evidences of Christianity numbered thirty-five in 1897 and twenty-eight in 1898. This study is not generally elected by the young women. In 1897 two-thirds were young men; in 1898 five-sixths were young men. The classes in the Greek New Testament numbered fifty-four in 1896, and in 1897 forty-one. The classes in Quaternary Geology numbered thirty-four in 1896, and twenty-nine in 1897—the young women numbering respectively eleven and eight. The classes in Harmony of Science and Revelation have numbered respectively fourteen and ten. Thus, in the course of the two years covered by this report, two hundred and forty-seven pupils have come under my instruction. The interest manifested in the work is encouraging.

Of the outside work done during the past two years, mention may be made of the preparation of a fourth edition of the "Ice Age in North America," which continues to sell both in this country and in Europe. Jointly with Mr. Upham I have also prepared a volume, containing 407 pages, of a scientific and general character, upon Greenland and the adjoining regions of the North Atlantic. I have also given a third course of ten Lowell Institute Lectures in Boston, an elaboration of which into a volume of 362 pages has just been published by D. Appleton & Co., and is meeting with a very gratifying reception both here and in Great Britain. Besides this, I have published numerous articles in the scientific and literary journals, and in the *Bibliotheca Sacra*, which I have all along continued to edit, and which has largely increased its circulation during the period — four-fifths of its subscribers being outside of Oberlin's ordinary constituency. I have also given many public lectures in various places, meeting everywhere a public which it is desirable to make favorably inclined to our educational work.

My geological explorations have been much limited by the failure of the proposed plan for raising the Cleveland Professorship. Still, I have spent considerable time and private money in carrying on investigations in the gravel deposits of the Upper Ohio and the Delaware rivers. The results are recognized as of great importance in determining the question of man's antiquity on this continent, and have been very widely noticed.

Yours respectfully,

G. FREDERICK WRIGHT.

REPORT OF THE DEPARTMENT OF THEOLOGY.

To the Chairman of the Faculty :—

SIR: In accordance with the plan proposed to the Trustees at their June meeting and accepted by them, the work in Theology has been extended and laid out as a five-hour course for two years. The first year's work in Philosophy of Religion is elective for the middle class in the Theological Department and for seniors and graduate students in the College Department. It takes up the fundamental inquiries in metaphysics, theory of knowledge, ethics, and philosophy of religion, which are essential to a unified view of the world. In this philosophical survey it is attempted to take account of the whole man, volitional and emotional as well as intellectual, and to give full weight to æsthetic, ethical, and religious data. The course is based, in its earlier part, upon Lotze's Microcosmus and Outlines of the Philosophy of Religion; and consists, in its later part, of a careful discussion of the bearing of evolution upon philosophy and religion, based on Le Conte's Evolution and its Relation to Religious Thought, and Schmid's Theories of Darwin. The best of the later literature on this subject is discussed. The work of the first year is intended rather as a supplement than as a basis of the work of the second year. It deals with the philosophical and scientific relations of Christian doctrine, and aims to secure for the student some freedom and independence in critical thinking, and an acquaintance with the fundamental philosophical problems that must be faced by every man who really desires to think the world through and to be a thoughtful leader of men. This course is given in Peters Hall, and is open to seniors and graduate students of the college department. During the current year this course has been elected by eight middlers from the Theological Department and thirty-two seniors in college. It seems likely to accomplish well the aims sought in its planning.

The work of the second year is devoted strictly to theological inquiry, and presupposes the courses in Biblical theology, history of doctrine, and apologetics. The first part of the course is given to a careful critical discussion of the most important theological movements of the present day. It seeks from the student himself a critical appreciation, favorable and unfavorable, of Frank's System of Christian Certainty, representing the conservative school of Germany; of Pfleiderer's Philosophy and Development of Religion, volume 2, representing the liberal school; of Ritschl's Instruction in the Christian Religion, representing the Ritschlian school, and of the theological portions of Fairbairn's The Place of Christ in Modern Theology. A similar critical appreciation is then undertaken of a number of the great creeds of the church: the Apostles' Creed, the Nicene Creed, the Athanasian Creed, the Form of Concord, the Second Helvetic Confession, the Arminian Articles, the Thirty-Nine Articles of the Church of England, the

37

Westminster Confession of Faith, the Burial Hill Declaration, and the Commission Creed of 1883. It is believed that this plan not only stimulates the student to independent thinking and secures both a broader and a deeper knowledge of theological questions, but also proves directly helpful to the student's own constructive thinking. The second part of the course is distinctly constructive, and is built immediately upon the results of Biblical theology. It aims to state every theological doctrine in terms of personal relation and in full light of the person and teaching of Jesus as the supreme revelation of God; and the meaning of the doctrine for life is held continually in mind. The confirmation of religious experience and of the historical and philosophical inquiry is then considered, and the attempt thus made to give to Christian theology its place in a really unified view of the world. Ex-President Fairchild's Elements of Theology is used for this part of the course, not as a text for recitation, but as a basis for discussion. The course is open only to members of the senior class in the Theological Seminary and to graduate students of the College Department.

As the present senior class in the Theological Seminary had already pursued theology with President Fairchild, this year's work was not required from them. All the seniors except one, however, elected it as a four-hour course, the other member of the class taking Theology I. instead. The course has also been taken by one graduate student in Philosophy from the College Department. The hope is earnestly cherished that the Chair of Theology may gradually be recognized as a real university chair, and the work offered by it as a natural elective for graduate students in the College Department, as in English universities. The placing of the Systematic Theology proper in the senior year of the Theological Seminary course, and opening it only to students of that year, it is hoped will make possible a notably high grade of work and furnish a natural conclusion to the student's own constructive thinking, upon a broad basis of preparation in Biblical, historical, and apologetic lines. One of the sore needs in theology is larger library facilities.

The brief course in the Elements of Theology given each year to the seniors of the College Department has been taught by me again this year. President Fairchild's book has been used as for some years past, and serves as an admirable compend for such a course. The theological questions arising have been frankly discussed, and the course has been followed with apparent interest and profit by the class. The course is a one-hour course through two terms, and is required for seniors.

The courses in English Bible in the College Department have always been carried as extra work by some members of the faculty. Of late this work has fallen exclusively upon Professor Bosworth and myself. Professor

Bosworth is giving the freshman course this year, and on account of a change in the sophomore schedule the regular sophomore course is postponed a year. It is not thought, I believe, by either students or faculty, that the students have suffered in their Biblical work. But the classes have had to be necessarily very large, and Professor Bosworth would agree with me, I am sure, in saying that it would be a great gain to both the College and Theological Department if a regular chair in the English Bible could be established. Oberlin certainly ought not, even apparently, to lag behind any other college in either the quality or extent of its Biblical courses. No man can do as extra work what a regular professor giving his full time might accomplish.

My own philosophical work has been reported upon in connection with the Theology. I have asked Associate Professor MacLennan to make an independent statement of his courses in Psychology, Pedagogy and Philosophy. Both of us give courses of lectures this year in Psychology before the Kindergarten Training School and arrangements are pending for a course of ten lectures before the public school teachers of Oberlin, Elyria and Lorain. The proceeds of the public school lectures are to be devoted to the further equipment of the work in Psychology. Only Dr. MacLennan's skill in arranging his experimental work makes it possible to offer the advanced course in Psychology this year. No friend of Oberlin should fail to notice the extension of work in Psychology and Pedagogy.

Respectfully submitted,

HENRY CHURCHILL KING.

REPORT OF THE SLAVIC DEPARTMENT.

To the Chairman of the Faculty :—

SIR: It gives me pleasure to report a year of exceptional progress, both in its quantity and quality, of the work of the Slavic Department. The number of students is ten—five Bohemians, four Slovaks and one Pole. The studies pursued have been Inductive Logic, Apologetics, Systematic Theology, Bohemian Syntax, and English Old Testament. With the exception of the last, all these branches are taught in two languages—English and Bohemian. The classes are unusually large, and the quality of work and grades of attainment unprecedented. One student, who is in his senior year, is taking select studies in the classical course altogether, studying the Greek New Testament, Homiletics, Elocution and Sociology. He will be our only graduate this spring, though next year we expect to graduate four. Another student is completing his preparation for the classical course in

39

College and Academy, while a third is doing excellent work in Greek Exegesis in connection with his regular work in the Slavic Department.

A Theological Club meets once a week to discuss more fully various philosophical and theological themes, under the leadership of the principal of the department. The Seminary method is employed at these meetings as far as practicable, the aim being to give the students a wider acquaintance with theological literature, both English and Bohemian.

Owing to the increasing difficulty of collecting the necessary funds, the financial condition of the department has never been more embarrassing. We are at present over one thousand dollars in arrears. The early and adequate endowment of the Slavic Department cannot be too strongly urged.

Respectfully submitted,

LOUIS F. MISKOVSKY.

REPORT OF THE ENGLISH COURSE IN THE THEOLOGICAL SEMINARY.

To the Chairman of the Faculty :—

SIR: There have been enrolled in the English course this year seventeen students. Last year there were twenty-four. Five graduated last May, and three will complete the course next commencement.

There have been given in these two years the following courses: Church History, four courses in English Bible, Evidences of Christianity, Logic, Psychology, Ethics, Elocution and Rhetoric, Systematic and Practical Theology and Homiletics. The English course has not recited with the Classical course except in President Fairchild's Theology. There has been no friction between the courses.

It is greatly to be regretted that this course must be abandoned at the conclusion of this year because of lack of funds with which to carry it on. The faculty and friends of the course have paid current expenses for three and a half years, and in addition have reduced the debt about a thousand dollars. Such is the record for the hard times. However, the faculty feel that they can no longer be responsible for funds. Those in the course now will be allowed to elect some studies from the Classical course to complete an equivalent of the English course. They will then be graduated from that course. They will make sixty-four who have graduated from it since its beginning.

Respectfully submitted,

J. F. BERRY.

REPORT OF THE ACADEMY.

To the Chairman of the Faculty :—

SIR: During the last few years the colleges have been demanding more from their candidates for entrance. This demand is not simply for more work, but for better work, and the burden which it imposes falls largely on the secondary schools. These schools, for the most part, welcome the new situation and are eager to meet the demand. This can only be the case, however, as they are equipped with better and more experienced teachers. The securing and holding of these teachers necessitates greater permanence in their positions and the payment of salaries more on a par with those paid instructors in colleges. Probably for some years to come Oberlin Academy cannot pay the most of its teachers salaries that will induce them to hold those positions for any great number of years. If it is to do first-class work, however, it must have a group of teachers not only whose appointment is permanent, but whose salaries are such that they can afford to hold these positions permanently. There are at present among its teachers two or three whose services it can in no case afford to lose. It seems only just that the salaries of these teachers should be increased.

For the last two or three years the numbers in the Academy have remained about the same, but they are decidedly less than ten years ago. This situation seems due not simply to the hard times, but to the genuine improvement in the high schools in the state. Thus, while the numbers in the high schools are larger, those in the academies are usually smaller. There are, however, in the small country towns, where there are no high schools, many boys and girls who ought to have a thorough education, and who would manage to secure it if their attention were properly directed to its advantages. They have in them the stuff out of which to make not simply scholars, but men and women of high character. To seek out these young people, who are likely otherwise to grow up without education, to to lead them to desire this education, and to help them to open for themselves the way to acquire it, seems a particularly wise task for Oberlin to take upon herself. She can thus not only add to her number of students, but also help forward distinctly the cause of education. This enterprise calls for a man who, for the present can give almost his whole time to this work of visitation. The right man is in sight, and can be secured whenever the money to pay his expenses is in hand.

Respectfully submitted,

JOHN F. PECK, Principal.

41

To the Chairman of the Faculty :—

SIR: Work in the Conservatory of Music has been going on since my last report very satisfactorily in general. During the first four years of this decade we were favored by a constantly increasing attendance. This increase reached its culmination in 1894, when we enrolled 720 students. During the last three years, however, there has been as constant a falling off in attendance, which, I think, is principally due to the financial condition of the country. Since the receipts of the Conservatory are dependent entirely upon tuitions paid by students, this falling off in numbers has been accompanied by a corresponding decrease of income; but by close economy we have been able to keep our expenses slightly under our income, and thus have been able to reduce certain advances that were made by the College some time ago. We hope that the return of prosperity to the country will bring a larger attendance, and so enable us to go forward without materially crippling our present teaching force.

There has been slight change in our faculty of instructors recently. In 1896 Mr. and Mrs. Hall, who had been with us for four years, were compelled, on account of ill health, to withdraw. The attendance at the time was not such as to demand the immediate filling of their places, and they have remained vacant since, although at this time the services of Mrs. E. G. Sweet became available for a limited amount of teaching. The Conservatory faculty has decided to recommend the appointment of Mr. W. T. Upton as instructor in Pianoforte, to begin active service in the fall of the present year. Mr. Upton was graduated from the Conservatory in 1893, and from the College (Classical course) in 1896, since which time he has been studying in Vienna, Austria, where he has been a pupil of the celebrated pianoforte teacher, Leschetizky. If the appointment meets with the approval of the Board of Trustees, we shall look for excellent things from him.

In June last the Conservatory graduated three young men and five young women, and at the coming commencement we shall probably have a class of nine to present for graduation.

During the last year, in our Artist Recital course, we have given our students the opportunity of hearing nine recitals, all by artists of a high order, among whom are M. Alexandre Guilmant, the celebrated organist from Paris; Mr. and Mrs. Henschel, from London; the Kneisel String Quartet, of Boston; Mr. Seidl's Orchestra, from New York; Mr. Henri Marteau, the French violinist, and others. By these and other means we endeavor to supplement the work of the instructor and elevate the ideals of our students, and give them a more thorough preparation for their life work.

The instruction given in the Conservatory differs little from year to year, and still there are some phases of our work which plainly show growth. In the Department of History a grade of work is being done which, so far as I know, is hardly to be equalled in any similar school in this country. In the earlier terms of the work in Theory, a course of a very exhaustive nature is being developed, in teaching students to think and hear more intelligently, that is of far-reaching importance. It has been attempted elsewhere only in a cursory and superficial manner.

In the other departments of Pianoforte, Organ, Singing, Violin, and nearly all the orchestral instruments, our teachers are doing a grade of work that is fairly comparable only to the best that is to be found anywhere. The trend of influence on the part of our teaching force is emphatically along the lines of solid musical development.

Respectfully submitted,

F. B. RICE.

Treasurer's Statement.

1897.

Treasurer's Statement.

To the Board of Trustees of Oberlin College:—

The Treasurer of the College submits his Annual Statement for the year ending August 31, 1897, as follows:

The funds separately invested are:

	PRINCIPAL.	INCOME.
University Endowment (part of)—		
University houses and lands....................	$ 18,626.00	$ 3.01
Construction account—Baldwin Cottage	13,470.31	191.37
" " Talcott Hall............	14,750.77	1,861.44
C. G. Finney Memorial Fund—		
Mortgages	65,878.14	3,762.46
Straus Fund—		
Oberlin real estate...........................	40,000.00	2,500.00
Foltz Tract Fund—		
Bonds..	546.93	24.85
Totals	$153,212.15	$8,343.13

The other Funds are invested as a whole. A summary statement of these investments with the net income thereof, is as follows:

	PRINCIPAL.	INCOME.
Notes and mortgages	$558,551.75	$33,188.06
Stocks, bonds and collateral loans	66,743 48	5,382.74
Real estate..	204,657.03	332.30
Advances to sundry accounts......................	23,106.35	
Cash in banks.....................................	2,784.73	195.54
Cash in Treasurer's office	493.84	
Totals of general investment..............	$856,337.18	$39,098.64
Totals of special investments	153,212.15	8,343.13
	$1,009,549.33	$47,441.77

The above investments are stated in detail, beginning at page 64 of this report.

In compliance with the instructions of the Board of Trustees properties not before valued have been entered on the books as follows:

The Plumb farm in Iowa has been placed in Real Estate account at $16,000.00, the estimated value when the farm was given to the College. A corresponding Ralph Plumb Fund has been entered as a University fund.

The Chapin insurance policies have been entered in Suspense account at a nominal value of $800.00, the dividends on these policies at present being about 6% on the above amount. A corresponding sum has been added to the Endowment Fund of the Theological Seminary.

The Toledo lots and the Button land in North Dakota have been put in Suspense account at a nominal value of $1.00 each, the same amount being added to University Endowment.

The West Virginia oil land has been entered as a special investment at a nominal value of $25.00, the same amount being added to University Endowment.

The village lots in Port Huron have been put in Suspense account at a nominal value of .$1.00, and the same amount added to the Ross Fund.

The Burrell coal in Illinois (undeveloped) and the Burrell house and lot in Oberlin have been placed in Suspense account at a nominal value of $1.00 each, and the same amount added to the Burrell Fund.

The Cross property in Minneapolis has been entered in Suspense account at a nominal value of $1.00, and the same amount added to the Fairchild Professorship.

The net income of the general investments ($39,098.64) has been divided at the rate of 4.8% among the funds to which they belong. The fraction ($69.55) was credited to the University account.

The following summary shows the income and expenses of the University, College, Academy and Theological Seminary:

	RECEIPTS.	PAYMENTS.	SURPLUS.	DEFICIT.
University	$ 9,319.52	$23,435.82		$14,116.30
College	39,798.33	34,378.81	$5,419.52	
Academy	13,387.03	15,468.22		2,081.19
Seminary (Theol.)	10,940.98	11,709.31		768.33
	$73,445.86	$84,992.16	$5,419.52	$16,965.82
		73,445.86		5,419.52
Balance showing deficit for the year	$11,546.30			$11,546.30

48

Gifts have been received during the year as follows :—

From J. E. Ingersoll, $100.00 for current expenses.
From E. A. West, $100.00 for the Library.
From Professor King's Training Class, $13.68 for the Library.

For beneficiary aid in the Theological Seminary, from—

F. H. Richardson	$ 10.00	J. N. Smith	$ 75.00
Mrs. Rebecca Webb	100.00	Pilgrim Church, Cleveland	53.36
James C. Strout	25.00	Second Church, Oberlin	246.46

For the support of the Slavic Department in the Theological Seminary from—

Mrs. F. A. Mather	$100.00	A. I. Root	$ 20.00
Miss Anne Walworth	950.00	J. Odell	25.00
C. F. Olney	100.00	R. F. Smith	10.00
S. P. Harbison	50.00	Miss F. S. Mather	150.00
J. E. Ingersoll	25.00	Marcus Lyon	50.00
Hower & Higbee	20 00	Mrs. S. N. Riley	10.00
H. C. Lane	10.00	C. F. Greenough	20.00
Thomas Rhodes	10.00	Mrs. Sarah Branch	25.00
Mrs. Alfred Stone	50.00	Cong. Church, Braddock, Pa.	30.00
Cong. Church, Elyria, O	100.00	Pilgrim Church, Cleveland,O.	25.00
Central Congregational Society, Brooklyn			50.00
A "Friend" in Michigan			75.00
Ohio W. H. M. U.			300.00
New York W. H. M. U.			210.00
Michigan " "			3.60
Through the Congregational Education Society			60.85
From unknown donors through T. Y. Gardner			263.00

For the support of the English Course in the Theological Seminary, from—

E. W. Andrews	$ 10.00	A. H. Currier	$ 25.00
D. H. Richie	20.00	Sydney Strong	65.00
H. J. Wilkins	10.00	C. L. Hyde	20.00
V. C. Smith	5.00	T. J. Collier	25.00
Dudley Allen	50.00	James Brand	50.00
W. A. Hutchinson	10.00	S. R. Wood	7.50
H. G. Husted	10.00	D. S. Husted	10.00
R. E. Hart	10.00	J. H. Palmer	2.00
E. L. Pickard	300.00	C. A. Coffin	50.00
E. I. Bosworth	15.00	G. R. Berry	10.00
C. W. Grupe	10.00	First Church, Oberlin	15.50

Total amount of these gifts for immediate use is $4,195.95, as is also stated on page 57 of this report.

✗   From J. G. W. Cowles, of Cleveland, O., $1,250.00 to found the Leroy G. Cowles Scholarship in the Theological Seminary.

✗   From E. A. West, of Chicago, $1,500.00, to found a scholarship in the College department.

✗   From the estate of Clarissa M. Smith, of Rochester, N. Y., $4,846.10 ($5,000.00 less the inheritance tax); her bequest to form a University Endowment fund.

✗   From Mary A. Springer, of Cleveland, O., real estate in Cleveland, O., valued at $5,000.00; now carries an annuity.

✗   From A. C. Dutton, of Eaton Rapids, Mich., $1,000.00; now carries an annuity.

✗   From J. H. Laird, of Hinsdale, Mich., $10.00; a subscription to the Fairchild Professorship.

The total amount of these gifts to capital account is $13,606.10 as is also stated on page 58 of this report.

The accounts hereinafter presented are:

First, a set of tables showing the current income and expenses of each Department in detail and a summary statement thereof, accounts relating to *general* objects or to specific objects of *general* interest being placed under the heading "University."

Second, a general statement of all receipts and disbursements by the Treasurer, except changes of investments.

Third, a list of all the Funds and Balances in the care of the Treasurer showing their amounts at the beginning and end of the year.

Fourth a classified list of the properties or assets in the hands of the Treasurer.

Fifth, a list of buildings, grounds, apparatus, etc., in use for College purposes and *not valued* on the Treasurer's books.

JAMES R. SEVERANCE, *Treasurer.*

Oberlin, Ohio, March 1, 1898.

THE UNIVERSITY

INCOME

From invested funds................................	$3,067.67
Real estate, rents...................................	2,503.01
From Boarding Halls................................	2,246.16
Rents of houses and lands not valued	335.06
Rent of Plumb farm................................	881.85
Finney Biography, copyright.......................	23.77
Physical Training Course, fees	162.00
Gift for current expense	100.00
Total income................................	$9,319.52

EXPENSE

Salaries—Administration...................$3,600.00		
Treasurer's office.............. 4,280.00		
Library 2,080.00		
Gymnasium .... 2,517.00—	12,477.00	
Clerks	422.77	
Stationery, printing and postage....................	1,734.48	
Advertising	332.37	
Fuel and lights....................................	1,232.76	
Buildings and grounds, care and repairs	2,527.73	
Annuities	2,500.00	
Men's Gymnasium..................................	388.34	
Women's Gymnasium	297.99	
Outside representation.............................	417.14	
Sundry taxes.......................................	253.29	
Sundry expense	647.45	
Payments on Lord, Cowles and Hinchman funds	204.50	
Total expense..............................		$23,435.82

Special Accounts—

Receipts.

Art School fees.....................................	$ 574.00	
Special instruction in Elocution	516.75	
Term bills, Teachers' Course, Woman's Gymnasium .	1,092.00	
Jennie Allen Nurse Fund	48.00	
Jones Loan Fund, loans returned	545.00	
" " " interest.........................	48.00	
Scholarship Funds, from investments	1,183.60	
Total receipts for special accounts...........		$3,522.35

Payments.

Art School	$ 574.00
Special instruction in Elocution	583.75
Teachers' Course, Woman's Gymnasium.............	909.23
Jones Loan Fund (loans made)	545.00
To holders of scholarship orders	1,041.75
Advances to scholarships repaid (part)	62.10
Oberlin Alumni Association	4.05
Total payments for special accounts.........	$3,719.88

THE COLLEGE

INCOME

From invested funds............................$16,941.24	
Term bills	20,372.10
Diplomas	457.76
Chemical Laboratory fees.........................	1,173.94
Botanical " "	293.59
Zoölogical " "	559.70
Total income.............................	$39,798.33

EXPENSE

Salaries $26,659.56	
Clerks	219.54
Stationery, printing and postage....................	85.74
High School Representation	218.58
Fuel and lights.....................................	911.56
Buildings and grounds, care and repairs	1,657.16
Chemical Laboratory.............................	1,172.89
Botanical "	296.67
Zoölogical "	541.36
Museum	363.00
Herbarium	172.73
Apparatus...	75.00
Alumni Dinner	265.87
Sundry expense	302.83
Trustee scholarships...............................	993.82
Avery scholarships	243.00
Oberlin College scholarships	199.50
Total expense.............................	$34,378.81

Special Accounts—

Receipts.

Scholarship funds from investments .... $ 408.00

Payments.

Expenses of Prof. Wright (research fund) ....$ 130.00
To holders of scholarship orders 360.00
Advances to scholarships, repaid (part) 24.00
     Total payments to special accounts..........—————— $ 514.00

ACADEMY

INCOME

Term bills $13,387.03

EXPENSE

Salaries $13,363.00
Clerks 181.42
Stationery, printing and postage..................   131.76
Fuel and lights...................................   307.68
Buildings and grounds, care and repairs 607.15
Apparatus 10.01
Sundry expense 13.20
Trustee scholarships..............................   854.00
     Total expense...................................—————— $15,468.22

THE THEOLOGICAL SEMINARY

INCOME

From invested funds...............................$ 9,696.00
Term bills 1,173.50
Diplomas 71.48
     Total income............................—————— $10,940.98

53

EXPENSE

Salaries	$ 9,800.00
Clerks	11.75
Stationery, printing and postage	99.96
Advertising	163.40
Fuel and lights	566.98
Buildings and grounds, care and repairs	1,026.02
Sundry expense	10.80
Outside representation	30.40
Total expense	$11,709.31

Special Accounts—

Receipts.

English Course, gifts for current expense	$ 730.00
Slavic Department, gifts for current expense	2,742.45
Scholarship Funds—From investment	804.00
" " Gifts	509.82
" " Loans repaid	110.00
Total receipts for special accounts	$4,896.27

Payments.

English Course, expenses	$ 730.00
Slavic Department, expenses	2,884.04
To holders of scholarship orders	1,417.50
Total payments for special accounts	$5,031.54

CONSERVATORY

INCOME

Term bills	$33,374.36
Interest on Reserve Fund	777.82
Rent of Williams house	167.85
Total income	$34,320.03

54

EXPENSE

Salaries $25,444.36
Library, etc 280.84
Stationery, printing and postage..................... 787.18
Advertising 352.70
Piano and organ tuning............................. 1,513.00
Fuel and lights...................................... 152.55
Janitors and engineers 1,846.45
Supplies and repairs................................. 1,248.09
Purchase of instruments............................. 1,016.68
Advances repaid (part) 1,678.18
    Total expense ....——————— $34,320.03

Special Accounts—

                                      Receipts.

Loan Fund, loans returned................................... $205.00

                                      Payments.

Loan Fund, loans made $228.00

LIBRARY

INCOME

From invested funds................................. $698.57
Dividend, G. T. Harvey Co 50.00
Term bills 1,157.29
From Conservatory.................................. 150.00
Private examinations 280.50
Registrar's fees.................................... 92.50
Books and supplies sold............................. 24.07
Gifts for current expense........................... 113.68
    Total ....——————— $ 2,566.61

EXPENSE

Librarian's assistant, clerks $656.50
Supplies 210.62
Binding books..................................... 492.73
Stationery, printing and postage.................... 29.00
Moving shelves, books, etc 16.99
Purchase of books................................. 1,285.68
    Total ....——————— $ 2,691.52

MISCELLANEOUS

RECEIPTS

Finney Memorial Fund, interest....................	$3,762.46	
Foltz Tract Fund, interest.........................	24.00	
Annuity Funds, interest...........................	5,471.74	
Total		$9,258.20

PAYMENTS

Finney Memorial Fund............................	$2,500.00	
Foltz Tract Fund (for tracts).......................	24.50	
Annuities	7,412.36	
Healey Fund (books)	15.52	
Total		$9,952.38

General Summary of Receipts and Payments by Departments.

University......................................	$ 9,319.52	$ 23,435.82
Special accounts..............................	3,522.35	3,719.88
College	39,798.33	34,378.81
Special accounts..............................	408.00	514.00
Academy	13,387.03	15,468.22
Theological Seminary............................	10,940.98	11,709.31
Special accounts..............................	4,896.27	5,031.54
Conservatory of Music...........................	34,320.03	34,320.03
Special account...............................	205.00	228.00
Library	2,566.61	2,691.52
Miscellaneous	9,258.20	9,952.38
	$128,622.32	$141,449.51

INCOME

Interest on notes and mortgages...................	$39,076.85	
" bonds and collateral loans..............	3,318.71	
" bank deposits	195.54—	$ 42,591.10
Dividends on Stocks:		
New England Loan and Trust Company........	270.00	
The G. F. Harvey Company	50.00—	320.00
Real estate, from rents, etc.; net receipts:		
Oberlin, gross receipts..............$8,491.38		
Less repairs and taxes........... 4,239.30—	4,252.08	
Plumb farm (Iowa), gross 1,058.34		
Less repairs and taxes.......... 176.49—	881.85—	5,133.93
Term bills:—		
University, from Physical Training Course......	162.00	
College	20,372.10	
Academy	13,387.03	
Theological Seminary..........................	1,173.50	
Library	1,157.29	
Conservatory..................................	33,374.36	
Woman's Gymnasium, Teachers' Course........	1,092.00—	71,292.28
Sundries:—		
Finney Biography, copyright...................	23.77	
Library fees, fines, etc	547.07	
Special instruction in Elocution	516.75	
Diplomas	529.24	
Laboratory fees—Chemistry.........$1,173.94		
Botany 293.59		
Zoölogy .... 559.70—	2,027.23	
Jones Loan Fund (loans returned)	60.00	
The May Moulton Memorial Fund (interest)	70.00	
Beneficiary aid returned (Theological)..........	110.00	
Conservatory Loan Fund (loans returned).......	205.00	
Sundry gifts for immediate use................	4,195.95—	8,285.01
Total income receipts....................		$127,622.32
Loan to General Fund		9,560.84
		$137,183.16

RECEIPTS EXCLUSIVE OF INCOME

Mary A. Springer Fund	$5,000.00	
A. C. Dutton Annuity Fund	1,000.00	
Leroy G. Cowles Scholarship	1,250.00	
E. A. West Fund	1,500.00	
Clarissa M. Smith Fund	4,846.10	
James H. Fairchild Professorship (additional)	10.00	
Total increase of permanent funds	—————	$13,606.10

Total receipts $150,789.26

PAYMENTS

Salaries:—

University	$12,477.00	
College	26,659.56	
Academy	13,363.00	
Seminary	9,800.00	
Conservatory	25,444.36—	$ 87,743.92

Clerks:—

University	422.77	
College	219.54	
Academy	181.42	
Seminary	11.75—	835.48

Stationery, Printing and Postage:—

University	1,734.48	
College	85.74	
Academy	131.76	
Seminary	99.96	
Conservatory	787.18—	2,839.12

Advertising and Outside Representation:—

University	749.51	
College	218.58	
Seminary	193.80	
Conservatory	352.70—	1,514.59

Fuel and Lights:—

University	1,232.76	
College	911.56	
Academy	307.68	
Seminary	566.98	
Conservatory	152.55—	3,171.53

Amount carried forward $96,104.64

Amount brought forward............................ $96,104.94

Buildings and Grounds, Janitors, Supplies, etc.:—
    University 2,527.73
    College 1,657.16
    Academy 607.15
    Seminary 1,026.02
    Conservatory.................................... 3,375.38—   9,193.44

Laboratories, Museum, etc...................................... 2,631.66
Gymnasia 686.33
Special Courses (all departments) 5,681.02
Scholarships and aid 6,087.07
Purchase of books... 1,325.70
Sundry advances repaid 4,548.03
Annuities... 12,412.36
Sundry payments.. 5,563.01

      Total payments $144.233.26

      Total receipts.............................. $150,789.26
      Total payments 144,233.26

Increase in Funds and Balances.................. $ 6,556.00
Increase from entry of properties not before valued   16,831.00

    Total, as is also shown on page 63 of this report $23,387.00

Funds and Balances in the care of the Treasurer.

August 31, 1896.

August 31, 1897.

UNIVERSITY.

$ 1,985.46	General Fund (so called)................	
58,793.37	Endowment $58,820.37	
17,514.89	Alumni Fund 17,514.89	
24,475.00	E. I. Baldwin Fund 24,475.00	
10,000.00	Henrietta Bissell Fund................ 10,000.00	
30,873.41	James H. Fairchild Professorship 30,884.41	
10,275.00	Walworth Fund 10,275.00	
38,000.00	Dickenson Fund 38,000.00	
	Clarissa M. Smith Fund.............. 4,846.10	
	Ralph Plumb Fund.................... 16,000.00—$210,815.77	

2,499.25	C. N. Pond Fund	2,494.21
6,927.90	Dutton "	7,840.44
96.17	Shaw "	92.79
2,999.90	Prunty "	2,993.90
195.94	Whipple "	191.34
296.91	Finney "	293.16
969.70	Davis "	936.25
95.97	Ryder "	91.58
8,907.30	Dascomb "	8,794.85
494.85	Warner "	488.60
64,530.50	C. V. Spear "	63,927.96
1,454.55	Gillette "	1,404.37
1,583.53	Butler "	1,563.56
484.85	Watkins "	468.12
436.37	Perry "	421.31
194.94	Seales "	189.30
95.97	Latimer "	91.58
6,498.05	Ross "	6,485.96
4,948.50	Gilchrist "	4,886.03
40,000.00	Marx Straus "	40,000.00
	Mary A. Springer Fund...............	5,000.00— 148,655.28

1,000.00	Cowles Memorial Scholarship	1,000.00
1,100.00	Dr. A. D. Lord Scholarship............	1,100.00
1,000.00	Mrs. Elizabeth W. Lord Scholarship.....	1,000.00
1,045.00	Hinchman Fund.......................	1,045.00— 4,145.00
	Amount carried forward	$363,616.05

$ 5,000.00	Lydia Ann Warner Scholarship ....$ 5,000.00	
1,000.00	F. V. Hayden Scholarship 1,000.00	
6,000.00	Avery Fund 6,000.00	
1,713.91	Finney Scholarship 1,698.91	
1,000.00	Howard Valentine Scholarship 1,000.00	
1,000.00	Caroline Scholarship.................. 1,000.00	
1,000.00	Talcott " 1,000.00	
1,000.00	Metcalf " 1,000.00	
1,000.00	Dodge " 1,000.00	
1,000.00	Dascomb " 1,000.00	
1,000.00	Bierce " 1,000.00	
1,000.00	Graves " 1,000.00	
500.00	Louis Nelson Churchill Scholarship 500.00	
200.00	Ann Lincoln Scholarship............... 200.00	
1,526.19	Jones Loan Fund 1,089.19	
1,250.00	Mary E. Wardle Scholarship............ 1,250.00	
	Unused income of above scholarships.... 94.75—	24,738.10

64,555.68	C. G. Finney Memorial Fund 65,818.14	
1,209.97	Jennie Allen Nurse Fund............... 1,257.97—	67,076.11
1,314.39	Balance credits, sundry accounts........	426.11

COLLEGE

67,889.88	Endowment........................... 67,889.88	
19,461.41	Dascomb Professorship................. 19,461.14	
50,000.00	Stone Professorship.................... 50,000.00	
55,881.37	Fredrika Bremer Hull Professorship 55,881.37	
30,000.00	Graves Professorship................... 30,000.00	
30,000.00	Brooks " 30,000.00	
29,709.89	Monroe " 29,709.89	
25,000.00	James F. Clark Professorship........... 25,000.00	
20,000.00	Perkins Fund 20,000.00	
25,000.00	Avery Professorship................... 25,000.00—	352,942.55
131.14	G. F. Wright Research Fund (balance).	1.14

Amount carried forward $808,894.81

	Amount brought forward.............		$808,894.81
$ 1,000.00	Jennie M. Williams Scholarship ....$	1,000.00	
6,000.00	Ellen M. Whitcomb "	6,000.00	
1,000.00	Flora L. Blackstone "	1,000.00	
500.00	Tracy-Sturges Scholarship..............	500.00	
	E. A. West Fund.....................	1,500.00—	10,000.00
	Unusued income of above scholarships ..	24.00	24.00

THEOLOCICAL SEMINARY.

33,481.88	Endowment..........................	34,281.88	
21,371.10	Finney Professorship	21,371.10	
8,935.84	Finney and Morgan Professorship	8,935.84	
25,000.00	Holbrook Professorship	25,000.00	
21,707.00	Michigan "	21,707.00	
4,750.00	Place Fund	4,750.00—	116,045.82
4,898.50	West Fund............................	4,783.63	
148.45	Hudson "	146.57	
5,236.44	Burrell "	4,471.43—	9,401.63
5,000.00	Lemuel Brooks Scholarship.............	5,000.00	
1,500.00	Jennie M. Rossiter Scholarship	1,500.00	
1,000.00	McCord-Gibson "	1,000.00	
1,000.00	John Morgan "	1,000.00	
1,000.00	Painesville "	1,000 00	
1,000.00	Oberlin First Cong. Church Scholarship ..	1,000.00—	
1,000.00	Oberlin Second Cong. Church " ..	1,000.00	
1,000.00	Anson G. Phelps Scholarship............	1,000.00	
1,000.00	Butler Scholarship.....................	1,000.00	
1,000.00	Miami Conference Scholarship...........	1,000.00	
1,250.00	Tracy Scholarship	1,250.00	
1,000.00	Sandusky "	1,000.00	
	Leroy G. Cowle: Scholarship...........	1,250.00	
700.00	Emerson Scholarship (part)	700.00—	18,700.00
949.41	Unused income of above scholarships ...		955.73
196.24	Balance credits, sundry accounts		39.13
	Amount carried forward		$964,061.12

Amount brought forward................ $964,061.12

CONSERVATORY.

$16,204.61	Reserve Fund........................$13,420.86		
583.50	Loan Fund...........................	560.50—	13,981.36

LIBRARY.

827.00	Class of '85 Fund.....................	827.00	
400.00	Cochran Fund........................	411.65	
500.00	Grant "	500.00	
50.00	Hall "	50.00	
100.00	Henderson "	100.00	
11,176.63	Holbrook "	11,176.63	
500.00	Keep-Clark Fund	500.00	
1,000.00	Plumb Fund	1,000.00—	14,565.28
445.69	Balance credits, sundry accounts		309.13

IN TRUST FOR PURPOSES NOT CONNECTED WITH COLLEGE.

547.43	Foltz Tract Fund......................	546.93
970,076.82	Total funds and balances	993,463.82

Total increase of funds and balances, $23,387.00

LIABILITIES.

15,950.00	Bills payable........................	2,500.00	
12,376.27	Deposits and personal accounts	13,585.51—	16,085.51
			$1,009,549.33

The following property represents the above named Funds and Balances and is answerable for the same.

Notes and Mortgages distributed as follows:

Cleveland $129,357.74
Akron 33,000.00
Oberlin 22,750.88
Sandusky 1,000.00
Burton 1,500.00
North Amherst...................   750.00
Kenton 1,500.00
Lorain 7,950.00
Toledo..........................   150.00
Talmadge........................   500.00
Farm lands in Ohio.............. 89,045.00
   Total in Ohio...............————— $287,503.62

Des Moines 5,150.00
Grinnell........................   5.000.00
Farm lands in Iowa..............   4,700.00
   Total in Iowa...............————   14,850.00

Grand Rapids.................... 21,775.00
Farm lands in Michigan 67,487.00
   Total in Michigan ....—————   89,262.00

Topeka 10,500.00
Salina..........................   2,000.00
Eureka 871.20
Hutchinson 5,000.00
Wabaunsee 350.00
Strong City.....................   480.00
Eldorado........................   4,000.00
Garnett 1,000.00
Farm lands in Kansas 105,395.68
   Total in Kansas ....————— 129,596.88

Duluth 23,300.00
Farm lands in Minnesota 2,550.00
   Total in Minnesota ....—— ——   25,850.00

   Amount carried forward $547,062.50

```
       Amount brought forward......        $547,062.50

Farm lands in North Dakota................    22,289.89
   "      "      South Dakota .............      800.00
   "      "      Nebraska .................    11,158.50
   "      "      Indiana ..................    30,625.00—  611,935.89

Stocks and Bonds:
   New England Loan and Trust Co. (preferred)..    4,500.00
   Streator, Ill., paving bonds.................    2,334.24
   Hutchinson, Kans., paving bonds.............   12,000.00
   Collateral loans ...........................   47,910.24—   66,743.48

Real Estate:
   Ashtabula (city property) ...........$   3,000.98
   Oberlin      "        "    ...........  61,379 68
   Sandusky     "        "    ...........   2,100.00
   Cleveland    "        "    ...........   5,000.00
      Total in Ohio..................——————    71,480.66

   Grand Rapids (city property)........    5,050.00
   Farm lands in Michigan ............   12,100.00
      Total in Michigan .............——————    17,150.00

   Topeka (city property).............   13,899.45
   Eskridge "      "       ............    3,000 00
   Hutchinson.......................     3,700.00
   McPherson........................      550.00
   Salina...........................    1,000.00
   Farm lands in Kansas ............. 101,411,34
      Total in Kansas ..............——————   123,560.79

   Fargo (city property) .............    4,100.00
   Farm lands in North Dakota........   10,365.00
      Total in North Dakota.........——————    14,465.00

   Farm lands in South Dakota ................    2,360.00

   Duluth (city property) ............    2,500.00
   Farm lands in Minnesota ..........    7,766.58
      Total in Minnesota .............——————    10,266.58

      Amount carried forward....................$239,283.03
```

Amount brought forward $239,283.03

Farm lands in Missouri 2,000.00
   "   "   Illinois 6,000.00
   "   "   Iowa......................... 16,000.00
     Total real estate............................—————— 263,283.03

Sundries:
Construction account Baldwin Cottage (loan)... 13,470.31
   "   "   Talcott Hall (loan)....... 14,750.77
Advances to Stewards of Boarding Halls 174.96
   "   Literary Societies 3.87
   "   Museum 1,464.75
   "   English Theological Course....... 1,027.40
   "   Slavic Department 203.05
   "   Scholarship and Beneficiary Acc'ts 759.05
Improvement to Straus Block 2,596.29
Unexpired Insurance........................ 2,255.50
Bills receivable and sundry accounts .... 18,041.57— 54,747.52

Loan to General Fund 9,560.84
Cash in Banks.............................. 2,784.73
Cash in Treasurer's Office................... 493.84— 12,839.41

$1,009,549.33

The following properties in use for College purposes are not entered in the foregoing list of assets, and are not valued on the Treasurer's books. The values given are reasonable estimates based on their cost and present condition:

Chapel	$ 20,000.00
Spear Library	30,000 00
French and Society Halls	14,000.00
Peters Hall	75,000.00
Finney Laboratoi	9,000.00
Cabinet Hall	5,000.00
Warner Hall	125,000.00
Council Hall	75,000 00
Sturges Hall	10,000.90
Talcott Hall and Furniture	65,000.00
Baldwin Cottage "	40,000.00
Lord Cottage " "	24,000.00
Stewart Hall	4,000.00
Keep Home	3,000.00
Other houses on College grounds	8,000.00
Library	50,000.00
Gymnasia and Apparatus	8,000.00
Physical and Chemical Apparatus	15,000.00
Museum	25,000.00
Botanical Collections	7,500.00
Musical Library	3,000.00
Musical Instruments and Apparatus	36,000.00
Arboretum	2,000.00
Athletic Grounds	700.00
Total	$654,200.00